Lauren
Wright
Douglas

A TIGER'S HEART

S·M·B

First published in USA by Naiad Press in 1992
This edition first published in Great Britain 1993 by
Silver Moon Books, 68 Charing Cross Road, London WC2H 0BB

Printed in Great Britain by
The Guernsey Press Co. Ltd, Guernsey, C.I.

ISBN 1 872642 12 8

A CIP catalogue record for this title is available from
the British Library

For Martha

About the Author. . .

Lauren Wright Douglas was born in Canada in 1947.
She grew up in a military family and spent part of her
childhood in Europe. She published her first short story
at age twelve in the school newspaper, and since then
has pursued a part-time writing career. To support this
avocation, she has been a high school English teacher,
a French translator, a college English instructor, a
creative writing teacher for gifted high school students,
a public relations person, and a grant writer. Lauren
moved from Oak Bay, Victoria, British Columbia to the
American Southwest some years ago where she now
lives with her partner and an ever-changing number of
cats. Lauren's second Caitlin Reece novel, *Ninth Life*,
won the 1990 Lambda Literary Award for Lesbian
Mystery.

'O tiger's heart, wrapped in a woman's hide!'

William Shakespeare, *Henry VI, Part 3*

FRIDAY

Chapter 1

Waiting at the seawall at Victoria's Inner Harbor, I found myself shivering, and not entirely from cold. The seaplane descending from the slate-colored sky was bringing a resurrected piece of my past. A skeleton I had buried deep and tried very hard to forget. As I waited, the drizzle which had been on-again off-again all day began in earnest. I turned up the collar of my jacket wishing I were anywhere but here.

The sky was the color of a day-old bruise and the sun, which had not graced us with its presence all that winter's day, prepared to expire somewhere behind the horizon. I forgave it. I felt more than a little moribund myself. Christmas was little more than ten days away, my birthday only six, and the advent of those two events had plunged me into my annual depression.

After the phone had rung at seven a.m. and I had heard the voice of a ghost, I had passed the hours doing busy work. Housecleaning, two loads of laundry — anything to keep my mind off what was about to happen.

But now the moment was at hand. The little red and white commuter plane skimmed over the pewter surface of the bay, then delicately touched its pontoons to the water, sending up twin arcs of lacy white spray. Settling like an ungainly bird, it wallowed to the dock, where two red-coveralled Air BC crew members were waiting to tie it fast. Then the door of the plane opened, and the passengers began climbing out onto the wet gangway. I knew that the plane held twelve people and I began to count. A party of six portly three-piece government types, two overdressed dowagers, two ordinary-looking young men in jeans and parkas, a young blonde woman in cords and a navy slicker, and a scruffy kid. The pilot and co-pilot emerged from the plane, closed the door and came running up the gangway into the little Air BC terminal hut on the dock.

My heart, which had been beating double-time, gave an alarming thud. I just couldn't believe it. She wasn't there.

I stood in the rain, wondering what in hell to do now. Go home, I guessed. If she was in as much

4

trouble as she said she was, she'd contact me again. Still, for some reason I couldn't name, I hesitated, the minutes ticking away. Below me, on the dock, the door of the Air BC terminal opened, and the kid I had noticed earlier came to stand outside in the rain. She was a girl of about ten, dressed in jeans and a blue nylon anorak, black hair braided. She took a long look around, then slumped against the closed door in eloquent disappointment. I looked at her for a long moment, squinting through the rain. She seemed so familiar. Then a bubble of recognition burst in my heart.

"Oh my God," I whispered, and started down the stone steps to the harbor.

The girl saw me coming and looked up, hefting her backpack. She was a skinny little kid with a fox's narrow, clever face, elfin eyes, and a gap between her teeth. My heart thudded again. She couldn't have looked more like her mother if she'd tried.

Sticking her chin out bravely, she demanded, "Are you Caitlin?"

"Yeah," I said. "Who are you?"

"Jory," she said. "Jonna's daughter."

"Of course," I said numbly. "You look just like her."

"Everyone says so," she agreed in a gravelly Kim Carnes voice.

I stood there for a moment wondering how in hell I was going to ask the next question. What do you say to a kid whose mother — your ex-lover whom you haven't seen in twenty-two years or heard from in eleven — calls you in the middle of the night in fear for her life, begging you to meet her?

How much, or little, did Jory know? Finally, I just came out and asked her, "So where's your mom, Jory?"

She didn't answer right away. "She's not coming," she told me at last. It was only then I saw the fear in her eyes.

I kneeled down so our faces were on the same level. "What's wrong, sweetie? You can tell me. I help people in trouble."

"Mom came to get me and we ran away. Just like we always do. But he found us. He always finds us. He beat her up, this time real bad." She closed her eyes, and I felt my own fear like a fist closing around my heart.

"Where is she, Jory?"

"Where I left her," Jory whispered, opening her eyes. "In a motel." Her eyes were hazel, just like her mother's. "She told me to run. So I did."

I tried to swallow but my mouth was too dry. "Tell me which motel. I'll call for help.

"No," she rasped. "She doesn't need your help now. She's dead. My mom is dead."

Chapter 2

I sat in the kitchen drinking strong coffee while my friend Sandy, a.k.a. Detective Sergeant Gary Alexander of the Oak Bay Police Department, took Jory's statement. Maybe I should have been in there too, holding the kid's hand or stroking her brow or whatever, but I'm no good with kids. And besides, I felt as though I'd been punched in the gut. Jonna dead? It wasn't possible. The two voices intertwined like the soprano and bass notes of a Gregorian chant. *Kyrie eleison:* Lord, have mercy. And then it was over. Silence. When he was finished, Sandy left her curled in a chair in front of the fire, my fat grey cat Repo in her lap. He took a phone call in my guest room-cum-office, then came to join me in the kitchen.

"Well?" I asked dully.

"South Van is on the scene," he said.

"Goody. The Keystone Cops."

He raised an eyebrow. "They're not such a bad lot." When I didn't reply, he sighed. "You know, there's a lot to this story that doesn't add up."

I tried to force my mind back on track. "Yeah? Like what?"

"The girl. Jory. Her story had a lot of inconsistencies. Either she's not telling us everything, or . . ." He leaned his large, hairy, tweed-jacketed frame against the fridge and studied the tops of his Oxfords.

"Or what?" I asked. "Hey — you don't think she made all this up, do you?"

Sandy shrugged. Irritated, I got up and closed the kitchen door.

"C'mon, Alexander. Give the kid a break. Does she have to tell you everything? I'm sure it's embarrassing to admit your parents beat each other up regularly. Cut her some slack."

Sandy sighed. "It's not that," he said, peering at me from the thicket of his eyebrows. "South Van didn't find the body."

"They *what*?"

"They didn't find the body," he repeated.

"Well, maybe they ought to look harder, damn it!"

"Caitlin," he admonished. "They *did* look. There

are clothes strewn around the room, things knocked about. But no body."

"But Jory saw it!"

Sandy sighed. "So she says."

"Oh come off it! Is that the way they want to play this — blame it on a kid's overactive imagination so they don't have to investigate?"

"I don't know, Caitlin. All I know is what I was able to get out of one of the blue suits who went out to take a look. She told me what I told you."

"Shit!"

"An apt summation," he agreed.

"Now what?"

He shrugged. "South Van will try to pick up the father for questioning. The manager took down his license plate when he was so daft as to park in a tow-away zone. But as far as they're concerned, no crime has been committed."

I bristled. "Jory's mother sent her to me for protection. The father is a wife-beater and for all we know, a child-beater, too! And she says she saw her mother lying on the floor, dead."

"Yes, that's what she says," he agreed.

"I'm getting a little tired of that particular tune," I warned him.

"Mmm," he said.

After I had calmed down a little, I asked, "So how do you read it?"

"If he killed her, then he moved the body."

"A delightful thought. What if he didn't?"

"South Van checked the hospitals — none of them has any record of her. So if she was injured, either she was able to walk out of there or he took her against her will. If she wasn't injured —" He shrugged.

"What's that mean?"

"She may have just walked away. Caitlin, these domestic disputes —"

"Don't be so patronizing! We're talking about a woman who was so terrified of what her husband might do to her that she sent her *kid* to me for protection."

"She did that," he agreed.

"So?"

"So nothing. This isn't my case," he reminded me gently. "And I don't want to speculate any more about why things don't add up. You'll just bite my head off."

"Sorry," I said. "I feel like arguing, I guess."

"Are you going to be all right?" he rumbled in his Scots burr. "You look a little green around the gills. Someone has to take care of the child in there but I'm beginning to suspect that someone ought to take care of you as well."

"Nonsense," I said mechanically. "I'm an adult. I can take care of myself."

He cocked an eyebrow but wisely said nothing.

"Her mother was ... my best friend," I said by way of explanation. "This is tough."

"That it is," he agreed softly. He sighed. "I'll call you if I hear something."

"Thanks," I said and walked him to the front door.

And that left me alone with Jory. I squared my shoulders and went in to face her. She was hugging Repo, her face buried in his gray pelt. He looked up at me with a silent meow as if to say, "What gives?" but made no other protest.

"How about a hot bath, some clean pajamas, and supper?" I asked brightly, perching on the sofa arm.

Misery in her eyes, she looked at me once and nodded. I had no doubt that she had seen exactly what she said she had. What was the matter with Sandy anyhow? So there was no body. So what? There was undoubtedly an explanation if anyone cared to look hard enough.

"C'mon, then," I said, holding out my hand. She took it, and I led her into my third bedroom, the one I keep nice and neat for all those guests I've never had. I put her backpack on a chair by the dresser and went off to get her bath running. When I came back, she was standing in exactly the same spot, although she had taken off her anorak, folded it neatly, and put it on the bed.

I was having a very hard time with all this. Part of me wanted to throw back its head and howl like a dog for Jonna; that part of me wanted, too, to be left alone to get roaring drunk. Perfectly understandable, I thought. But a mean-spirited part of me wanted Jonna alive so I could excoriate her — so I could say all the things I'd been too damned noble to say when I walked away from her more than twenty years ago. And that part of me, the part that wanted to scream and gnash and call Jonna every rotten name in the book, wanted also to beam this child onto another planet. What shudder in the loins had engendered her? And why the hell was she standing in my *home*?

Ah, shit, I told myself. You told Sandy to cut the

kid some slack — you could do the same. None of this is her fault.

"I don't have any clean pajamas," she said in a low, croaky voice. "In fact, I don't have any pajamas at all. Or any underwear. Or really anything." She crossed to the chair and took her backpack, unzipping it and emptying it on the bed. Out tumbled a dirty navy sweatshirt, a wool sweater, a pair of tan cords, a couple of hardback books, some T-shirts, a spiral-bound notebook, a blue leather cat's collar with ID tag still attached, a picture in a silver frame, a cigar box held together with a rubber band, and a hairbrush. "That's it," she said.

"Hmmm," I said, as if considering the matter deeply. "I could lend you some pj's — I have some sweats that I left in the dryer too long. They ought to fit you."

She considered this, her lips a thin line. "They'll just be a loan, though."

"Absolutely," I said. "I'll just leave the sweats in the bathroom. Okay?" Reluctantly she nodded. "And help yourself to dresser drawers and so on. Make yourself at home." She tilted her head to one side, a gesture so like her mother's that it hurt. "You're my guest," I explained.

When she didn't move, or speak, I sensed there was something she wanted to say, something that was more significant than dresser drawers or borrowed pj's. I sat on a corner of the bed and patted the mattress. "Want to talk?"

She nodded and after a moment sat tentatively beside me. "I heard what he said, about the ... about my mother not being found. So what's going to happen?" she asked in her husky voice.

Good question, kid. Madame Caitlin will consult her crystal ball. "I don't know," I said wearily.

"What if the police never find her? Or him?"

"They probably will," I reassured her. "They're good at that sort of thing."

She shook her head. "I don't think they'll find *him*," she said with a reasonableness that was chilling. "He's good at getting away. He always does." She looked at me sidelong. "And he's always found us, no matter where we went. He's good at that, too." She turned to reach behind her for the cigar box. Slowly she peeled the elastic band off it, slipped it onto her wrist, and opened the lid. There were some documents inside, a thin pile of photos, a couple of newspaper clippings and, I saw with surprise, a compact roll of money. "This was my mom's," she explained matter-of-factly. "She called it our escape money. It was my job to keep it safe." She counted out five hundred-dollar bills and closed the box lid, securing it with the elastic band once again. I had a horrible premonition of what was coming next. "But there's no point in running away any more." I wasn't sure if she was talking to herself or to me. She laid the five hundreds on the bed between us. "My mom told me this is how much you charge to get started helping people." She looked at me with eyes empty of innocence. "Is it enough?"

I swallowed. "Enough for what?"

She seemed surprised. "Enough for you to find *him*."

"Sweetie, the cops will find him," I demurred.

She shook her head patiently. "They don't believe he killed my mother, so they won't try very hard, will they?"

I said nothing.

"Before, when they went looking for him, it was for wrecking cars or smashing windows. Now when he's done something *really* bad," she paused, then continued bitterly, "they're not even going to look for him very hard." After a moment, she asked, "Well? Is it enough? I can get more, if that's what you're worried about."

I felt sick. "No, that's not what I'm worried about."

"Well, what then? You don't want to work for a kid. That's it, isn't it?"

I shook my head. "No, that's not it."

"Well?"

I took her skinny little hands in mine. "Jory, you don't seem to have much faith in the police. But if I found your father, I'd just hand him over to them. It would amount to the same thing."

She looked at me as though I were a particularly slow pupil. "I don't just want you to find him," she said. "I want you to kill him. For what he did to my mom."

I felt a spider of fear walk across the back of my neck. "Of course," I said, trying to keep my voice steady. "Let me think it over, okay?"

She shrugged. "Okay."

I stood up. "Soap and towels are in the bathroom. Why don't I fix us something to eat?"

When I heard Jory splashing in the tub, I filled a pot with water and put it on to boil for pasta. Then I rooted in the cupboard, found a jar of Ragu,

14

and poured it into a saucepan. That seemed to take care of the necessary supper preparations. I stood, hands in my pockets, looking out the kitchen window at the dark sky, trying not to think of Jonna or Jory or Jory's monstrous offer. Jesus Christ. What had I done to deserve all this?

"I'll set the table," a croaky voice said behind me.

I turned. Jory stood there looking uncomfortable, sweats rolled up around her elbows and ankles, wet hair dripping on the floor.

I reached out to feel a tendril of hair and she shied violently from my hand. "Hey," I said softly. "Jory, it's all right."

She looked at me, eyes blazing, and I knew how much she hated herself for letting a stranger see her fear.

"C'mon," I told her, pretending cheeriness and optimism. "Let's get your hair dried. You'll have pneumonia otherwise."

To my relief, she followed me into the bathroom.

"Sit here, on the edge of the tub," I told her. She did, and I began to comb the tangles out of her long black hair. The comb hung up in something, and Jory grunted. "Sorry," I said, removing the comb and picking off the glob. At first I thought she had a piece of black gum stuck in her hair, and then I thought it might be pitch or tar. But with a stab of horror, I realized that the comb was hanging up on blood which had dried and caked to her scalp. The hair-washing and my vigorous combing had loosened it. And as I parted her hair for a look, I saw the extent of the injury — an area about two fingers long, just behind her ear. And it was bleeding now. My stomach heaved.

"Jory," I said, "We need to take care of this cut on your head. It's going to get infected if we don't."

Her shoulders sagged. "It'll be all right."

"I don't think so, sweetie. Hey, let's do this," I said brightly, handing her a towel. "Hold the towel on the cut. I'll dry the rest of your hair."

She nodded and I turned the dryer on MAX, ruffling her hair to make it dry faster.

As I lifted her hair to dry around the back of her neck, I noticed that my sweat top was just about falling off her skinny shoulders. I bent to tug it into place and as I did so, I noticed something else, something that made my skin prickle with horror: the kid's upper back was covered with white scars — puckered and seamed like a collection of obscene zippers. Someone had been abusing this kid for a long time. That made my decision for me. I wasn't going to play doctor. Late hour or not, Jory was going to get medical attention.

The phone interrupted me just as I was tucking Jory into my parka. I stopped to answer it and sent Jory on out to the car.

"It's Sandy," a tinny voice said.

"Where are you anyhow — Inuvik?" I asked irritably. I didn't want to hear what he had to say. I didn't want to hear him tell me that they'd found Jonna's body.

"Might as well be," he snorted. "I flew to the mainland to see for myself. South Van isn't treating it as a crime scene, so it's not secure."

"Assholes!" I exploded.

"Hmmm," he equivocated. "The room's due to be cleaned tomorrow, so I snooped around. I did find some blood — in the shower drain. But that doesn't necessarily mean anything — someone could have cut themselves shaving. Of course, the clothes have been gathered up — they're in the motel manager's office." He sighed. "There's definitely no body — here or in any of the other rooms. And none of the other motel guests heard anything."

I looked out the window at Jory waiting by the car. "So what's the official verdict — the kid made it all up?"

"We won't know until we see a copy of the police report. I'll get on that tomorrow."

He sounded dead tired, and I relented a little. After all, he'd flown across the channel for me. It wouldn't kill me to express some gratitude. But the fact that even he doubted Jory still irked me. "Thanks, Sandy."

"I'm going to fly back to the island now," he told me. "I'll be home in about an hour if you want to talk."

"No, get some sleep. You can call me once you have the police report. And thanks again." I tried to inject some warmth into my voice, but I found I couldn't. So I just hung up.

Chapter 3

I sat in Maggie Kent's living room reading a three-year-old copy of *Organic Gardening*, trying my best not to heed the panic that yammered in my brain. One of my oldest friends, Maggie is a back-door physician. She can't practice legally any more — she had her license yanked in the sixties for performing an abortion on a thirteen-year-old who had been raped by her uncle. A pair of fundamentalist assholes, the kid's parents got cold feet at the last minute and blew the whistle on Maggie, putting *finis* to a promising medical career.

She'd only escaped prison by a whisker. But Maggie's clients don't give a rat's ass about all that. True, our visits aren't covered by Canada's wonderful free medical plan, but Maggie's waiting room is never jam-packed full of people imagining they're at death's door, either. Maggie allows plenty of time for patient visits, charges what you're able to pay, and has been known to take her fee in trade — the new furniture in the living room was a payment from a grateful patient. And the best thing about Maggie is that she'll see you day or night. I couldn't think of a better place to take Jory.

Tossing the magazine down on the couch, I got up to pace. I felt the way I always imagined Alice must have felt, just as she'd stepped through the looking glass: what the hell was going on? Only a day or two ago I was a modestly successful, moderately jaded private investigator; now I was a basket case. Worse than that, I was a basket case with a ghost from the past (who might or might not be dead, and who, if I was honest with myself, I wasn't sure if I wanted back in my life alive and kicking) and with a kid on my hands whose story nobody believed. Nobody but me. A kid for God's sake! What on earth was I supposed to do with a ten-year-old? And a homicidal one at that! And exactly why had Jonna sent her to me, anyhow? My deeply and carefully buried feelings about Jonna were surfacing like the zombies in *Night of the Living Dead* and I feared they would be equally violent.

Jonna and I had been classmates in our last year of high school — I was the class jock and Jonna was the class outcast. Jonna was *metis* — mixed blood, half Indian and half white — and in those days in Southern Ontario you might as well have been a leper. And as if it wasn't bad enough that Jonna was *metis*, she lived with her mother's family on the reservation, and slept above their pool hall. And she *looked* like an Indian, dammit.

The first time I saw her was the first day of class in Grade Thirteen. I was a new student — my family had just returned from seven years spent on military bases overseas — and I was more than a little nervous about fitting in to a big Canadian high school. Our homeroom teacher had assigned us places in alphabetical order and when he called my name, I took my seat behind a muscular, auburn-haired boy with classically handsome features named Kirk Ratliffe. As I sat down, I heard the teacher call out another name.

"Rowan," he intoned in a bored voice. "Jonna."

A tall, dark-skinned girl detached herself from the group of students waiting to be assigned their places and walked down the aisle toward me. I know I just stared. Her hair was longer than shoulder length, and so black and sleek it shone. She wore a white Oxford-cloth button-down shirt, cuffs rolled up, and a navy skirt which emphasized her slenderness. Tall, straight, and regal, she strode down the aisle toward me, eyes on the back wall.

"Make much money this summer?" Kirk whispered as Jonna approached his desk. He stuck his legs out in the aisle, effectively blocking her path. "So what's the price this year, Pocahontas?"

I couldn't believe what I was hearing.

Jonna stopped and, taking her eyes off the back wall, looked at him as though she were examining a particularly loathsome bug. Her eyes were hazel, with flecks of gold around the iris. She looked like Joan Baez. I thought she was the most beautiful girl I had ever seen. "If you were a man, you wouldn't have to ask," she told him enigmatically. "Now move your legs, little boy."

Horrified, I blushed to the roots of my hair. The students sitting around us tittered and guffawed, and I realized this must be only the latest scene in what was clearly a sordid and continuing drama between these two.

To my surprise, Kirk did move his legs and Jonna walked past him to take her seat behind me. As I watched, Kirk's ears turned a deep red and I guessed he was smarting under Jonna's ridicule. We stood as the public address system played "God Save the Queen" and in the noisy shuffling that ensued as we took our places again, Kirk turned to Jonna.

"I'm going to make you sorry you said that," he whispered hoarsely, two fiery spots of color blazing on his cheeks. His angry glance passed over me once, then dismissed me as someone of no importance. Shit! This was *my desk* he was threatening her across. Did he think I was deaf and blind?

"Oh, I'm sure you'll try," Jonna told him, her voice betraying not a hint of concern. I was impressed.

The bell rang then, and we gathered up our books for our first class. Because I wasn't sure of where to go, I got lost and by the time I found the right room, everyone had selected seats. There was only one seat left — in the far back corner. Just in front of Jonna. I sat through the introduction to

King Lear — the play we would be studying that term — with my mind on Jonna, not on what our teacher was saying.

I didn't see her second or third periods — she took algebra and physics, while I took geometry and zoology — but I finally caught sight of her again in the cafeteria at lunch. She was sitting at a table by herself, eating an apple and reading a book. After I had bought a sandwich, I took my tray to her table.

"Mind if I sit here?" I asked.

She looked up curiously. "No."

I put my tray down, unwrapped my sandwich and began to eat. "I'm Caitlin Reece," I told her after a few moments of uncomfortable silence.

"I know," she said, not looking up from her book.

I was so embarrassed I wanted to drop through the floor. Jonna closed her book, placed it carefully on the table in front of her, and leaned across the table to talk to me.

"Caitlin Reece, what planet are you from?" she asked.

I blinked. "What?"

She sighed. "Listen, it's not too late. Take your stuff and go sit somewhere else. Over there, for instance." She shrugged a shoulder in the direction of a table full of laughing young people. "Those are the popular kids. The ones a cute new student ought to hang out with. Do yourself a favor and walk over there. Introduce yourself. Ask the girls where they get their hair done, where they buy their clothes. Smile. They'll make room for you."

"What are you talking about?" I asked, hurt and confused.

She looked at me for a long moment. "You really don't get it, do you? I'm a *metis*."

"A *what*?"

She raised her eyebrows. "*Have* you been on another planet?"

"I've been living in France for seven years."

She smiled. "Same thing. I'm *metis* — mixed blood. My mother was a full-blooded Indian. My father was a white man."

"Oh," I said. "So what?"

"We're Canada's niggers," she said cruelly. "Now do you get it?"

"Yeah," I said. "I get it."

"So go," she said. "You can still be popular, still have friends, but you have to go now. Don't think they aren't watching."

I looked over to the table Jonna had pointed out, and dammit, they *were* watching. And right in the middle of them was Kirk Ratliffe. I think that was what decided me. That, and the fact that I knew, too, what being an outsider felt like. When you move every eighteen months, you learn that real fast. "I think I'll stay," I said, and held out my hand across the table. "Let's start over. Hi there. My name's Caitlin Reece."

Something moved behind her eyes, and for a moment it was like looking through a dappled forest glade into the sunshine beyond. "I'm Jonna Rowan," she said, taking my hand. "Pleased to meet you."

Under the disapproving gazes of our classmates, we shook hands. It was one of the most foolhardy things I've ever done, but caution never has been my watchword.

"Earth to Caitlin," Maggie Kent called, breaking into my memories.

"Sorry," I said, turning to face her. A smiling, blue-eyed woman in her fifties, her unfashionably white hair cut in an old-fashioned pageboy, she had been my doctor for seven years.

"Let's have some coffee," she said. "We need to talk. Robin took Jory downstairs to her apartment. They're making a pizza." I thought hungrily of the now-cold pasta and Ragu sitting in pots on my stove.

"Good," I said.

Twenty-five to Maggie's fifty-five, Robin was Maggie's live-in physician's assistant. She had been brought to Maggie's one night five years ago when she wandered in to the local women's shelter, dazed and battered, her collarbone broken in a domestic dispute. She never left Maggie's. Curly-haired, freckle-faced, relentlessly cheerful and possessed of a mind-boggling array of domestic talents, Robin was Maggie's right arm.

I frowned. "Jory, is she . . ."

"It's not a bad cut," she said. "It bled a lot, though. Head wounds usually do. Should have been attended to when it happened. I cleaned it up and put in a couple of sutures. She said she didn't remember how she did it."

I raised an eyebrow.

"Yeah," Maggie said. "She's got dandy bruises on her left upper arm, and her back is a mess. Lots of old scars and some fresh abrasions."

"I saw her back," I said. "Jesus, Maggie, what do you suppose happened to her?"

She shrugged. "Hard to tell for sure. But my guess is that someone grabbed her by the upper arm, held her, and beat her. With something moderately heavy that had an edge to it. A board, say."

She spooned coffee from a can into an old metal coffeepot, filled it with water, then returned the coffee can to the fridge, closing the door gently. "I don't see many child abuse cases," she said. "They usually pass through the ERs. The parents know full well that everyone's too busy there to play sleuth."

I wasn't sure how to ask the next question. "Do you think that the beatings are all that happened to Jory?"

Maggie turned a burner on underneath the coffee pot and gas ignited with a dull *whoomp*. "You're asking me was she sexually abused. I'd guess that she was. But I don't think we'll get Jory to tell us voluntarily."

"Why not?"

"Kids seldom tell. Guilt, shame, fear of the attacker, fear of not being believed." She shrugged. "It's a huge and ugly problem."

I thought of the scars on Jory's back. What other scars did she carry — unseen scars, scars on her soul? "How huge? Tell me about it."

Maggie looked at me over the tops of her glasses. "The statistics say one in three girls. Maybe one in thirty boys. Child sexual abuse tends to go unreported, so there's no way of knowing for sure. But the reported cases show child sexual abuse is common. Ninety-eight percent of the attackers are men, and the victims are mostly girls."

"Jesus." I put my head in my hands.

"Yeah. It's an unfortunate fact that we live in a society where violence against women and girls is made to seem attractive. Advertising, the media, pornography, the music industry, hell, permissive parents, hell, even our language — they all suggest to boys and men that it's okay to beat up on girls and women. Then the law all too often lets the bastards get off scot free." I decided not to object. Maggie had a point, even if she did generalize a bit too much. She broke off and sighed. "Jory has scars on the backs of her hands, too, over the knuckles. I figure that when she was beaten, she laced her hands together over her head to protect her face and ears, and either knelt or curled up in a ball, letting the blows fall on her back."

I swallowed, feeling ill.

"Black?" she asked, taking two mugs out of the cupboard.

"Yeah," I answered distractedly.

She poured coffee and handed me a mug that said LIFE IS A TERMINAL CONDITION.

We sat at a little oak table in the corner of her cozy kitchen. The walls were papered in a cheery floral design, and the cupboards had been recently painted yellow. Robin's handiwork, I guessed.

"We live in a rotten world," she said. "Our planet is polluted, and we've mortgaged the health of future generations for cars and video games. So it seems perfectly consistent that men foul the lives of girls. It reflects a terrible selfishness, a demand that *their* needs be met, even at the cost of their own children. We've been receiving the same message for twenty centuries: women, children, and animals don't count. Only men count." She fell silent for a moment, then seemed to shake herself. "Sorry. The sexual abuse of little girls is something I'll never get used to."

"How do you handle it?" I wanted to know. "The rage, your sense of . . . helplessness."

She grinned crookedly. "Much to my chagrin, I've become a do-gooder in my old age. I try to help women heal themselves. One at a time."

"Like Robin," I guessed.

"Yeah. Like Robin. So, how have you been?" she inquired shrewdly.

"Well enough," I said evasively.

Maggie snorted and raised a hand to touch a swatch of hair over my left ear. I'd been shot there last year and when the hair grew back, it'd grown in white. "This is nice," she said sarcastically. "A knife? A tire iron? A two-by-four?"

"A gun," I told her. "My own." Seeing that a little more explanation was necessary, I sketched in the details of the picture. "Wielded by someone who was pretty unhappy with me at the time."

"You're one lucky lady."

I thought about the woman who had shot me, and my heart twisted. "Yeah, that's me. Lucky is definitely my middle name."

"Come off it. You *are* lucky. It goes along with your Celtic blood — must be in the genes. But you can't dissemble worth a damn. You're looking pretty frayed around the edges if you ask me."

"Don't start with me, Maggie," I sighed.

"Okay, I won't. I just want you to know that if you need anything, well . . ."

Oh Maggie, I thought bleakly. *What's wrong with me can't be fixed by anything in your pharmacopeia. It's like the coffee mug says: life is a terminal condition.* "Thanks for the offer," I said lightly. "If I need pills or potions, I'll keep you in mind."

"So tell me about the kid," Maggie said.

Ah yes. The kid. My would-be employer, for God's sake. "Well, until yesterday, I didn't know she existed. She's the daughter of ... an old friend in trouble. Jonna Rowan. She called me and asked for help. Said she was coming in on the two-fifteen seaplane. She didn't. Instead she sent Jory."

"Hmmm," Maggie said, patient, waiting.

I decided to tell her the rest. "As far as I can tell, Jory and her mother lived on the run. They were always just one jump ahead of the kid's father." The kid's father. I heard myself say the words, but I didn't want to think about what they meant. "Then yesterday he got lucky. He caught up with them in a motel on the mainland." I raised my eyes from the polished grain of the oak table to Maggie's face. "Jory says she saw ..." I swallowed, forced myself to say it. "She says she saw her mother lying on the floor, dead. And so she ran."

"To you."

"Yes. To me."

"How did she know to come to you?"

"Because her mother told her to," I said through clenched teeth.

"What are you most angry about Caitlin?" Maggie asked after a moment, putting one hand over mine.

What the hell. I told her the truth. "Angry? I'll tell you why I'm angry. Because someone would do this ... this *thing* to a little girl. Because a mother and her kid had to run for their lives from a maniac who just wouldn't leave them alone. Because the mother never once called me for help until it was too late. Because the police don't believe Jory's story. Because a little girl wants her father dead. And because, God damn it, I know the son of a bitch who's Jory's father and it's killing me! He was a shithead when he was a kid, and he's a shithead now." I shook Maggie's hand off and grabbed the edge of the table. I felt as though my head would explode unless I let some of my anger out. "I saw Jory's name written on a tag on her backpack. Jory Ratliffe. Ratliffe! Jonna married the bastard! and she had his *kid.* Jesus Christ!" I wanted to throw back my head and bay at the moon.

"Your Jonna," Maggie guessed.

A bubble of grief burst in my throat. "Yes," I cried. "My Jonna. She married him. Kirk fucking Ratliffe. And there's a better-than-even chance that he's killed her."

At home, alone, after the Ragu and pasta were thrown out, after the cats were fed, after the bathroom was cleaned up, I suddenly had nothing to do. I wandered around the living room as if it were an unfamiliar place, picking things up and putting them down until I realized that I was pacing. Fleeing. Or trying to. But memory cannot be fled. It can be repressed for a while, but it cannot be eluded forever. I had buried Jonna deep, but evidently not deep enough. I closed my eyes ... and with a stab of panic realized I couldn't even visualize her face. And try though I might, I couldn't immediately call to mind any of the good memories. Distressed, I tried harder. And what surfaced was a curious thing ...

It is spring. I have known Jonna for nine

months, a sufficient gestation period for most things. We are walking in the woods on a trail that leads to her grandmother's cabin. This is Indian land, Iroquois land. Officially it is reservation land. There is almost no one alive in Jonna's grandmother's clan who can remember any other way of life. But her grandmother can. She can remember that the Iroquois call themselves Ganiengehaka or "people of the flint." Her Iroquois name is Katsitsaroroks. It means "gathering flowers." The French who conquered the Iroquois bastardized her name to Fleur. Fleur lives by herself in a cabin that she and her husband built with their own hands. Even though he is many years dead, she will not move into the reservation "town." She wants to die here by the river, she says. I admire her for this.

"This is dumb," Jonna says, with an all-too-familiar pout. During the months I have known her, she has begun to display what I find to be a dismaying contempt for the customs of her people. "Fleur's a little crazy. You don't have to participate in this. Hell, she could do it by herself."

"I thought she said she needed two maidens to help her?" I say, pulling her hair playfully, trying to lighten things up. These days, I never know how far I can go with Jonna. She is bored with me one minute, angry and accusing the next. "We're the only maidens I know," I say lightly. "The class virgins."

Jonna tosses her black hair and laughs, and her laughter disturbs me more than a little. Actually it is the subject that disturbs me. Sex. During the nine months I have known her, I have begun to suspect that Kirk Ratliffe's crude question posed last September may have a grain of truth to it. But because I am in love with Jonna, I am able to ignore or rationalize those things I do not wish to deal with.

Jonna's grandmother waves to us from the little clearing where her cabin stands. Fleur is wrinkled and toothless, no longer tall and straight. She supports herself on a heavy carved stick and shades her eyes, watching us walk from the woods into the clearing.

The forest floor is spongy underfoot, dark and steamy with moisture that the sun draws from it. My arms and the top of my head are warm and I look up through the apple-green buds of the oak trees, to a sky that is no longer winter blue. It is spring, I am seventeen and in love. I feel that all things are possible.

"Today is the day," Fleur tells Jonna. "Did you look for the signs?"

Jonna huffs, showing how bored she is by what she calls "all this Indian stuff." But I am not. "Yes," I answer at once. "All week I've been looking. Today, this morning, I went out and looked at the oak trees behind my house again." I couldn't help grinning. "The leaves are just like you said — the size of squirrels' ears. So it's time. Right?"

"Hee, hee," Fleur laughs. "You think you are one of the Onkweh-Onweh. Non?"

My grin fades. I know I can never be one of the Onkweh-Onweh, the real human beings. "No, Mother. I know I am not."

She cocks her head to one side and looks at me with shrewd bird's eyes. "But you could be. You could be adopted by someone in our clan."

"Fleur, please," Jonna says in exasperation. "Caitlin has her own family."

"Hee, hee," Fleur laughs again. "Does she now?"

I feel a shiver down my spine. How can Fleur know how out of place I feel in my own family, how important I think all this "Indian stuff" is? In the beginning I thought this marvelous heritage would be something Jonna and I could share. But as Jonna grows increasingly disdainful of her culture, I find myself more and more fascinated by it. I know this irritates Jonna, but I am unable to resist the siren song of her people's history and customs. Or Fleur. Perhaps she reminds me of my own grandmother, Meadbh, transported from her family's ancestral farm in Wales to die in a small white room in winter, in an Ottawa hospital. The difference, though, is that Meadbh said yes to the forces that sought to move and change her. Fleur says no, much to Jonna's disgust.

"Come," Fleur says. "I have everything ready."

"This is stupid," Jonna whispers.

"Hey," I say soothingly. "We're just helping an old lady plant her corn. No big deal."

Outside the cabin, we wait. Eventually Fleur emerges, three pieces of white birchbark held in her cupped hands. "Come close," she says. We do. She looks into Jonna's eyes, seems to find something lacking, grunts, and turns to me. "You," she says, "you will carry the spirit of Onenhste."

I blush to the roots of my hair. It ought to be Jonna doing this, carrying the spirit of the Corn

Maiden, not me. "No," I protest. "Mother, don't you think —"

She shushes me with a gesture and hands me a scrap of birchbark. I look down. In it are seven fat kernels of corn. With an angry exclamation, Jonna slaps my hand and the corn falls to the ground. Fleur hisses and bends to retrieve them. I look at Jonna in horrified disbelief, frightened by her disapproval, frightened by her violence.

"I'm leaving," she tells me. "Fleur can do this alone. She has for years. You can come or you can stay."

I pause, undecided. I had thought there was nothing more important to me than being with Jonna, but suddenly, I want her to go away. I am embarrassed and angry at her treatment of her grandmother. "I'll stay," I say.

She blinks, then turns on her heel and runs into the forest. I want to call after her, to beg her to stay, but my throat closes over the words. What she did was needlessly cruel and I find that I am glad she is gone. I refuse to imagine what will happen later — the silences, the angry words, the quarrel, the reconciliation. It is a pattern that is all too familiar to me by now. I let her go and turn back to Fleur.

"Come," Fleur says, handing me the birchbark and the corn kernels. We walk toward the little field she has prepared for the corn. "She will leave us, that one will," she says, referring to Jonna. "She will leave you, and leave all those who love her."

"Why?" I ask, my throat full of tears.

"I cannot say," Fleur answers. "Perhaps she has been touched by Atotaroh, the Crooked Man. But

33

you will come to us when Jonna leaves this earth."
She smiles. "You will come bringing us a gift."

My scalp prickles. "A gift? What kind of gift?"

"A gift for our clan. For Okwaho, the wolf clan."
She reaches into the capacious pockets of her skirt
and brings out a small buckskin bag. She places it
in my free hand. "You will know what to do with
this when the time is right. Put it away, now."

I put the buckskin bag in the pocket of my jeans
and go with Fleur to plant corn.

A log popped in the fireplace. The fire had
burned down while I sat remembering. Fleur. And
Jonna. Things went from bad to worse that day. The
pattern that had become all to familiar to me —
angry words, quarrel, and reconciliation — was
finally broken. This time there was no reconciliation.
Much later, walking home past the pool hall where
Jonna lived with her aunt's family, I saw Kirk
Ratliffe's little red car drive up and, improbably,
Jonna get out. To say I was stunned would be an
understatement. It was one of the true shocks of my
life, and it took perhaps a full minute for my brain
to make sense of what I was seeing. Jonna with
him? But why? I recall vividly that as the car drove
off she turned to look at me where I stood, dumb as
a post in the middle of the muddy lane. She
regarded me critically, then smiled the smile of a cat
who's been into the cream. A superior smile, full of
secrets. I wanted to drop through the earth because
I knew what that smile was saying. We'd talked
about what Kirk wanted from her many times, and

she'd sworn that she'd die before she gave it to him. For the first time in my young life, I was pierced by an anguish so sharp I thought it might kill me. I walked past her without saying a word. She leaned against the doorframe, hands in her pockets, and let me go.

Walking home, I tried to blame Jonna, couldn't, and so decided to blame myself. What had I expected, anyhow? I was a queer, a dyke, a lesbian. I had had the temerity to fall in love with my best friend, and the singular lack of judgment to tell her about it! I remembered how she had received this news (with grave understanding) and how she had responded (with a sisterly kiss). She understood, she said, and although she didn't feel the same, she wanted me to know we could still be friends. I had been so grateful I wept.

Now, more than twenty years later, recalling all this adolescent angst, I snorted, disturbing Repo, who stretched and yawned hugely beside me. Absently, I stroked his gray suede pelt.

I hadn't seen Jonna again that year. She dropped out of school. For my part, I took my final exams, won a scholarship, and moved out of town to attend college, all in a grief-filled daze brought on by Jonna's betrayal. I was unable to savor my accomplishments. It was not until the end of September, when I was well into my freshman year, that I believed I might live, that I might get through one day without thinking of Jonna.

But October put an end to all that. October 5. That was the day that Jonna came back.

I closed my eyes. I really didn't want to think about this anymore tonight. If I allowed myself to continue, I'd never sleep, and I had a busy day planned for tomorrow. These were old wounds; scratching them could wait.

"Whaddya say, fat boy?" I asked Repo as I got up to spread ashes over the dying coals.

"Mmmrap," he muttered.

"I'll bet you don't know that almost forty percent of cat owners confide in their cats."

He opened one yellow eye at this revelation.

"Aha. A flicker of interest. Well, what I want to know is how many cats talk back. Hmmm? And do they do so out of politeness or a genuine desire to share in the conversation? Now that's a much more interesting question."

"Yap," he agreed, rolling into a ball and falling asleep again.

I headed for my bedroom, turning lights off as I went. And though I had resolved not to think about Jonna, my sleep was plagued by dreams of a raven-haired woman who drove off laughing in a red sports car with a good-looking man, leaving me standing in the middle of the rutted road, choking on my tears.

SATURDAY

Chapter 4

Next morning, as I prepared for work, I gave myself a pep talk. *Try to put Jonna out of your mind. Dead or alive, she'll be found. You'll tell Jory no, you can't help her. And in the meantime, there's nothing you can do. Get on with your life. You're not seventeen now — you're an adult. You have control over how you feel. Don't resurrect ghosts. What's over is over.*

Brave words when the sun's shining outside your window and life is going on everywhere around you. But in the hours between midnight and dawn, however, courage is not as easy to come by. Especially when one's id keeps sending inappropriate dreams. So finally, nothing but an immoderate amount of Scotch had helped me put Jonna out of my mind. Consequently this morning I felt as though my head had been served, set, and spiked in a hotly-contested volleyball match.

After two aspirins and a long shower, I toweled dry and surveyed my visage in the steamy bathroom mirror. I didn't look quite as haggard as I felt, which was more a testament to good genes than good living. I grimaced, examining my dental work, then closed my mouth and took a long hard look at myself. Curly red-brown hair, gray-green eyes, pale skin and freckles — a typical Celtic lass. But in my case, the years had added several furrows of frown lines and more than a few wrinkles around the eyes and mouth. I didn't know if I liked them or not. Were they signs of incipient maturity or reminders of a life lived too hard? One of my friends was fond of saying that after forty it's patch, patch, patch. Great.

I gave my hair a final toweling and walked to the closet to survey my paltry wardrobe. What *does* one wear for an interview with the Crown Prosecutor, anyhow? I snorted. Seven years ago, I wouldn't have had to agonize over this — hell, I *worked* for him. Caitlin Reece, barrister and solicitor, attorney for the Crown. One of the Good Guys. Quietly efficient in my wool suits, matching silk shirts, pearls, and Italian leather shoes, I'd put quite a few of the Bad Guys away. But quite a few was never enough. To hell with it. This wasn't a costume party; it was an interview. I decided to dress as myself. I pulled on a pair of beige wool pants, an oyster-colored silk shirt, a Fair Isle vest, gave my almost-dry hair a cursory brushing, and pronounced myself ready.

"I don't know why I'm doing this," I announced to the cats, who had lined themselves up beside their food dishes. "Hell, I didn't enjoy working for him when I worked for him, if you know what I mean."

"Nup," said Repo, eyes riveted to the can of Mixed Grill I held in my hands.

I scooped the contents of the can into three dishes, and two of my cats — rotund gray Repo and blind tabby Jeoffrey — politely began their morning meal. Repo licked my hand before he started eating — a gesture that never failed to endear him to me, and I returned what I imagined to be his show of feline affection with a scratch behind the ears. The boys were about halfway through their meal when a truly hair-lifting growl from the pantry brought them up short.

Repo looked up at me for protection.

"Forget it," I told him. "You guys have to work this out yourselves. All the books say not to intervene."

"Yang," he said miserably, regarding the pantry door with evident dismay.

He didn't have long to wait. A tiny apricot and white cat emerged from the pantry, sashayed over to where Repo sat in front of his food dish and prepared to stare him down.

"Grrrairrr," the intruder rumbled.

"Oh for crap's sake, knock it off," I told Pansy. "We know how big and tough you are. Why can't you eat your own food and let them have theirs?"

"Ffffssss," she said.

"Nuh," Repo intoned in dismay, suddenly recalling that he had urgent business in the living room. He nuzzled Jeoffrey on the way past, and the two hustled themselves out of the kitchen, giving The Cat From Hell a wide berth.

True to form, Pansy had lost interest in Repo's food as soon as Repo had lost interest in protecting it. It was the confrontation she enjoyed. "You should have been a lawyer," I told her, dropping a frozen bagel into the toaster. While I poured coffee, Pansy selected a spot of sunshine in the middle of the kitchen floor, hoisted a back leg and began to wash her nether regions. As I sat down at the kitchen table, she gripped her back leg with both her front paws, swiveled her head 180 degrees like Linda Blair in *The Exorcist,* winked one yellow eye solemnly, then resumed her toilette.

Who can figure cats? I don't acquire them; they acquire me. Half-feral Pansy had been left for me by a former client who swore she would return for her once she had found a job up-island. Uh huh. That was six months ago. Repo was rescued by friends from the psych lab at U Vic — the only survivor of a cageful of cats who perished when the animal keeper went on a sudden two-week holiday. And Jeoffrey had been tossed into a dumpster in a pillowcase one cold fall night, the butt of an unspeakably cruel joke at a cosmetics lab, a joke that left him blind. Oh sure, I could have taken them to the SPCA shelter, but what would their chances have been? Who would have wanted to adopt a fat neurotic gray guy who checks the cupboards every other day and pulls out his fur when the stack of cans gets too low? Or a runty blind tabby who runs when he smells shampoo? Or a cantankerous apricot and white lady with a chip the size of a litterpan on her shoulder? Adoption? Forget it. Somehow we all get along.

As I munched my bagel, I thought guiltily about Jory. Leave her with me overnight, Maggie had said. Maybe she'll talk about what happened to her. She can help Robin panel the library. I had readily agreed — maybe a little too readily. I *would* have to give the kid an answer — at least I'd have to pretend I'd taken her seriously. But hell, I had a million other things on my mind. This interview for one. My relationship with Tonia Konig for another. I did not need a kid underfoot. And certainly not a kid who thought I was a hired gun. If I was absolutely honest with myself, I'd have to admit that she scared me half to death.

I looked at my watch. Why the hell didn't Sandy call? Sometime during the night I had decided that Jonna alive or Jonna dead meant absolutely no difference to me. She had been as good as dead for more than twenty years as far as I was concerned and I had no intention of disinterring her now. The only complication was Jory. And I'd already decided on her disposition: Social Services. I didn't give a rat's ass if Jonna had sent her to me or not. I was not responsible for her. She could go straight from Maggie's to the Social Services Department. Kids were their business. As for Kirk Ratliffe, let the cops find him and put him away. Or not. Who did Jory think I was — an avenging angel? I had my own life to live.

Brushing crumbs off my vest into the sink, I grabbed my bomber jacket from the coat tree and hurried out into a December day numinous with sunshine. Pausing on the porch to take in a lungful of crisp winter air, I permitted myself a small rush of optimism. Things would turn out, I vowed. I would make them work, as I always had. I was still in control of my life. Everything was going to be fine. Just fine.

"You're looking considerably the worse for wear," I told Niall as I took a seat opposite him at a window table in the Laurel Point Inn's fancy dining room. I had taken a perverse pleasure in selecting this location for our luncheon interview because it was a ferociously expensive place that I otherwise couldn't afford. What the heck — the Canadian taxpayers owed it to me.

Niall MacPherson, Victoria's Crown Prosecutor, looked at me out of red-rimmed eyes. Beefy, red-haired, and bellicose, he had not aged well in the years since I'd worked for him.

"I can't say the same for you," he said appreciatively, putting the lie to Maggie Kent's observation. I tried my best not to preen. "You look, well, fit. Self-employment must suit you. You've cut your hair," he observed.

"A symbol of my emancipation," I told him.

"And you're wearing trousers," he said, a

persimmon-colored eyebrow lifted in implicit disapproval.

"A symbol of something else. As Dorothy Sayers said: 'If the trousers do not attract you, so much the better; I do not want to attract you. I want to enjoy myself as a human being.'"

"Hmmmm," he said, deciding wisely to drop the subject.

"Let's order," I suggested. "You can make your pitch while they're rustling up the grub."

We both ordered salads, followed by smoked salmon on spinach linguini in pesto. I had the raspberry chocolate mousse lined up for dessert, but decided to wait and see how the interview progressed before committing myself.

After the waiter had brought the salads — hearts of palm on a bed of radicchio with peppercorn dressing — and the requisite bottles of Perrier, Niall got right to the point.

"I want you to work for me again," he said.

I almost inhaled my radicchio. "Shit, Niall," I said in dismay. "When I quit seven years ago, I quit for good. I have absolutely no desire to come back."

He made an impatient gesture. "I know that."

"So why are we here?"

"Like I said, I want you to work for me again. Except this time you'll be doing freelance work."

"What? Since when did the CP's office hire freelancers?"

He frowned heavily. "I've avoided it during my regime."

My regime. Give me a break! He always talked like that, like the CP's office was his fiefdom. That was one of the things I liked least about him. Nevertheless, I put down my fork and listened.

"Things are changing, Caitlin. You saw that." He looked up at me with pale blue eyes. "You got out. Some of us can't make that break so readily."

I bristled. "It's not as if I retired to do macrame or raise orchids."

"I know what you do," he soothed. "My point is that some of us still believe in the system."

"Why?" I asked, curious.

He left off shredding the label of his Perrier bottle and said, "Why? Because we have to."

I felt a surge of sympathy for him, for all the Good Guys who feel that they must wear the pennant of Justice on their lances. Players on a losing team. "Probably so," I agreed.

"My staff . . . well, they know libraries, and books, and the courtroom. They're well prepared. The young ones are even enthusiastic." He sighed. "But we're drowning in a sea of cases. We can't make some of the most heinous charges stick because, hell's bells, we can't *prepare* them properly. There are too many of them and too few of us."

An all-too-familiar story. "So what do you want me to do?"

He sighed again. "As I said, my staff knows law books and precedents and courtrooms. But they don't know the streets. They don't know the world."

Ha. They didn't know where to dig up dirt was what he meant. "And you need someone who does."

"Yes. I need someone who does. I need someone who can *investigate,* not research. I need someone who knows how to run down the facts we need, the facts that are out there on the streets, not in the bloody law libraries. Caitlin, I'm at the mercy of a staff of clerks!"

I groaned silently. "Niall, I never want to set foot in that place again. I don't want to see them ... the guys you're trying to put away. I ... I can't."

"I know," he said, not unkindly. "And you wouldn't have to. You can fax me what you find, or phone it in, or send it by courier. You wouldn't have to come to the Courts. And you'd be working for me. I'd be the one giving you your assignments."

I breathed deeply. It was certainly tempting. "What about pay?"

"Invoice us. You'll be a consultant."

"Oh yeah? I charge private clients two-fifty a day for my services."

"Do you really?" he asked, eyebrows shooting up in surprise. After a few seconds of finger-drumming, he announced grandly, "Well, as I said, just invoice us."

I looked out the window. Where the opal-colored sky met the slate water was a silver band of brightness, all that remained of the sunny morning. Was there an omen there, a message? I forced my mind back to the business at hand. "Let me think it over, okay?"

He seemed cheered by this equivocation and immediately changed the subject, chatting now about people we both knew from my days spent working for him. Relieved, I joined him in getting caught up on who had married, divorced, had kids, or changed jobs. And as the business part of the lunch was over, and when the waiter disappeared with the remains of our entrees, I went ahead and committed myself. I ordered the mousse.

"We don't know how it's being done," Yvonne told me.

"But it has to stop," Malcolm said.

"How much do you figure has been stolen?" I asked.

Blond, blue-eyed, rosy-cheeked, Malcolm and Yvonne sat opposite me in the tiny office of the Oak Bay Natural Food Emporium and fretted. "About six thousand dollars," Malcolm said apologetically.

"Jesus H. Christ!" I yelled. "When you told me someone was dipping into the till, I figured you were down a few hundred. A thousand at most."

"Sorry," Malcolm mumbled.

Yvonne reached over and patted his hand. "Mal said you'd yell," she told me. "That's why we've been putting this off."

I held up my hands. "Okay. No more yelling. But how can you guys be so calm about this?"

Malcolm brushed a wing of blond hair out of his eyes. "We have no choice. Business has to go on."

I exhaled heavily and fished in my pocket for my notebook. "Give me the particulars."

"Well —" Malcolm started.

"It's —" Yvonne interrupted.

"I'm going to fetch tea," Malcolm said, leaping to his feet. "Yvonne, you tell it."

When the door was closed, Yvonne said, "Poor Mal. You intimidate him, Caitlin."

"Fiddle-dee-dee," I told her. "I'm all bluster."

"No, you're not. Not all. That's the part Malcolm is afraid of. And he's a nervous wreck, Caitlin. He hasn't slept the whole night through for almost a month."

Feeling chastened, I reached over and patted her hand. "I won't even raise my voice. I promise. And I won't say you should have come to me sooner, although you should have," I said pointedly. "So just tell me the story."

She smiled in evident relief. "Okay. As near as we can tell, it all started five months ago, when we bought the shop next door and expanded into it. That's when we started carrying all this kitchen stuff. Cookware, linens, glassware, cookbooks. And some local pottery and fiber art. It's been doing well," she said. "That's what had us so puzzled. Our stock is way down."

"But your bank account isn't way up," I guessed.

"Right."

"What does the register tape say?"

She shrugged. "I run it out at the end of the day. There's nothing wrong. What we've taken in matches what's in the till."

"Hmmm."

Malcolm backed into the office, a tray held in his hands. Yvonne got up and closed the door carefully after him. "Chamomile tea," he said, handing around mugs. "Good to calm the nerves," he added, with a meaningful look in my direction.

I sipped, vowing to be gracious. "Nice," I lied and forced myself to swallow. I guess I'm just old-fashioned, but I don't think the odors of flowers and freshly cut grass belong in a beverage. They seem better suited to the realm of personal grooming aids. Heck — give me a good cup of strong coffee any day. Still, I made the necessary appreciative noises. A small sacrifice for friends.

"Do you have the applications your employees filled out?"

They looked at each other shamefacedly. "Well, we didn't make them fill anything out," Malcolm said. "We just took their word for things. Where they'd worked. You know. We made a few phone calls. But that was all."

I groaned, remembering my promise.

"We've never had any trouble," Yvonne said. "Not in six years. And we've had quite a bit of staff turnover. You know, young people coming and going."

"We trust people," Malcolm said dejectedly. "We thought we were pretty good judges of character. I guess we were wrong."

"Not necessarily," I told him, trying my best to be gentle. "One bad apple in six years seems like a pretty good record to me."

He brightened at that.

"Okay, write down the names and addresses of your staff and anything else you can think of about them. How long they've worked for you, cars they drive, husbands and kids they have, hobbies, what they do in their spare time — that sort of thing."

"I'll do it," Yvonne said, tearing a sheet of paper off a yellow tablet on the desk.

"Um, we wondered," Malcolm said, "well, the thing of this is that our business insurance will only cover five thousand dollars of the thefts. So we're already in the hole. What's missing is close to seven

50

thousand," he confided. "I took inventory last week. It took two bloody days. As you know, we're not computerized."

"So you want this cleared up fast?"

He nodded miserably.

"How fast? Fast enough to fire everyone and hire new staff?"

"Caitlin!" he exclaimed, shocked. "We can't do that. The Labor Department would murder us!"

"Leave the Labor Department to me," I told him. "There are plenty of precedents for this sort of thing."

"Well, we can't," he said with finality, crossing his arms over his chest. "Gwendolyn's baby is almost due."

Deliver me from bleeding hearts.

"Caitlin, there's something else," Yvonne said.

"Yvonne, no," Malcolm pleaded.

"Yes, Mal," Yvonne said firmly. "I want whoever's doing this to be punished." Her mouth was set in a serious line.

"Yvonne," Malcolm said in horror.

"No, I do, Mal. It's not an eye for an eye. It's not like that. But I want it on their record. I want other people, other employers to know that this person can't be trusted. So they won't be taken in the way we were."

If the new employers even bother to check references, I thought unkindly. "Okay, listen up," I said. "Here's the quick way to find out who's robbing you blind."

"Not that firing thing," Malcolm said.

"No. No firing. What I had in mind was some hiring. An extra employee, added for the Christmas rush."

"But we don't need another employee," Malcolm said.

"An undercover operator," I explained. When no comprehension dawned, I took a firm grip on my patience. "A plant," I tried. Then, "A spy."

Their blue eyes became very wide. "Oh." They exchanged periwinkle glances. "Who?" they inquired in unison.

"Who? Why who else would I recommend for a dirty, low-down, sneaking job like that?" I said wearily. "Me, of course."

"But that's not what you want to do, is it?" Tonia Konig asked.

We were chopping wood in her back yard — me chopping, her stacking — and we were about halfway through the cord of cedar she had had delivered yesterday. The pieces were too big to fit in her woodstove and I had volunteered to reduce them to a nice, manageable size. My back was already telling me the offer hadn't been one of my brighter ideas.

"I don't know," I said, resting on the axe. "Digging up dirt for Niall would probably be a lot safer than what I've been doing for the past couple of years. And it would mean a steady paycheck."

"I can't believe you're saying this," she said, hands on hips.

"Well it's the truth, isn't it?" I swung the axe

and a hunk of cedar split with a satisfying *thock*. "I don't know if I want to do it, but it certainly has its merits." I didn't say so, but I knew that an offer of regular remuneration and fewer risks was something that halfway appealed to me. Maybe it was a function of turning forty, but the continued prospect of being vilified, kicked, clobbered, and shot was not a cheery one. Or maybe my disenchantment was merely a function of the approaching winter solstice — my birthday. Whatever the reason, I found myself unable to turn away from Niall's offer.

Tonia paused in her wood stacking and I knew she was looking at me. "You didn't like working for him when you were working for him," she said, sounding exactly like me. "You told me so."

I examined the axe blade critically. It could use a little sharpening. "I don't mind Niall," I said. "It was the futility of what I did at the CP's office that finally got to me. The Big Picture."

She jammed her hands in the pockets of her cobalt blue hooded sweatshirt and leaned back against the woodpile. "Do you think you'll be able to insulate yourself from that?"

I stood another log on end on my chopping block and got a good grip on the axe. "Maybe. Maybe not. I'd be dealing with the little picture, though. Self-contained assignments. Collections of facts."

"Facts that may or may not be enough to send accused wrongdoers to prison, Caitlin. And if they walk free, do you really think you won't blame yourself? You know: if only you'd tried harder, worked longer hours, talked to more people." She took her hands out of her pockets, stripped off her leather work gloves, and laid them carefully on top of the woodpile. "You'd be right back in the rat race again."

I swung the axe. With a satisfying *thunk* that I felt all the way to my shoulders, the log split into two pieces, then fell to the ground.

"You wouldn't be happy," she added.

I stood the axe beside the chopping block. "No," I told her, "but I'd be in one piece."

She raised an eyebrow. "I didn't think that was important to you."

"Of course it's important to me," I said carefully. "But it's not of overriding importance. Losing pieces of my hide, well, I don't like it, but it goes with the territory. Sometimes it's the only way to get things done."

"But?"

"But what?"

"What you said seems to be a subordinate clause. I'm waiting for the 'but.' And the next clause."

I took a deep breath. "But you don't like it much, do you?"

"Of course I don't like it much! Who would?"

"No one in her right mind."

"Caitlin! You're not thinking of going back to work for Niall because *I'd* like it better?"

"That's part of it. And part of it is that —" I broke off, groping for the right words. "It's people," I told her lamely.

"People?"

"Yeah. They ask for my help — hell, they pay for it — but they're never straight with me. At best they tell me something approximating the truth. At worst they just plain lie. Dammit, Tonia, they tie my hands. They won't let me do my best. It's as though —" I shrugged and stood the axe up by the chopping log.

"As though what? They really don't want help?"

"Sometimes I think that. I do. But that's so irrational. No, I suppose what's at the heart of it is that they don't want to be ... responsible. To participate. To help themselves. They seem to just want me to fix things." I sighed. "And I'm getting tired of being reminded that I really can't fix things. People in trouble, hell, their lives are like runaway trains. You can jump on board but you can't change tracks and you sure as hell can't stop them. Sometimes I think it might be smarter to stand back out of the way and let them go by."

"And you'd avoid all this if you went back to work for Niall."

"Yeah, I would."

She crossed her arms and examined the flagstone patio for a few moments. "I'll be honest with you. What concerns me most about what you do is not so much that in the course of things you have to take a few lumps. That's not it." She raised her eyes to look at me. "What worries me most is that you're ... a courage junkie."

"A what?"

"Maybe that's not the right expression, but it seems to me that what you do, what you really do, you don't do for your clients. You've said yourself that they tick you off with their lies and evasions. No, I think you do what you do for yourself. I think you do it because *you* need to do it. And I think that's why you won't go back to working for Niall."

"What on earth do you think I need to do?" I asked her.

"Oh, I don't know. Pull Satan's beard. Go toe to toe with the Forces of Evil. Spit in the eye of the devil. Conquer chaos." She shook her head. "Something like that. I don't understand what compels you to do this. All I know is that you do it."

"And?"

"And what?"

"That's a subordinate clause," I told her testily. "Let's have the rest."

"Okay. I'm afraid that one day this ... thing you do, this compulsion to say no to the bad guys is going to kill you."

"Ah," I said.

"Yes," she agreed.

"So you'd like me to stop."

"No."

"No?"

"No. I wish you'd never started, never *needed* to start, but no, I don't want you to stop."

"Oh."

"That still doesn't mean that I like or accept what you do. What it means is that I understand it. I just don't know if I can ... live with it."

"Well, that's fair enough," I told her.

"We have to be straight with each other, Caitlin. I don't want to change you."

"Good. Because I'm too old to change even if I wanted to."

"Caitlin, listen," she said. "There are very few

narratives for women's lives. Apart from the marriage plot, there are so distressingly few plots or patterns. And so few brave stories. There are dozens of quests available to men — just look at literature, it's full of men's adventures — but for women?" She shook her head. "So few. No, women if they want to achieve have to do something that men have never had to do. They have to write their own scripts. Make up their own stories. Invent themselves." She was quiet for a moment. "Just like you're doing. I wouldn't get in the way of that for the world. That's your quest."

I was silent.

"And me? Well, I'm a coward, you see. I don't want my heart broken when I learn that you died in some godforsaken place in the middle of the night for someone who ticked you off in the first place."

She looked at me intently, smoky blue eyes unreadable. The weather spared me the necessity of making a reply. A spattering of fat raindrops made us look up at the sky, which had turned a dismaying purple-gray at the horizon. A few more raindrops hit the patio and Tonia turned to put on her gloves again. "Let's quit for today. I'll take a load of wood inside and start a fire. Will you cover the rest with the tarp?"

"Sure. Go ahead." After Tonia went inside, I fussed around, sweeping up the wood chips, putting the axe in the tool shed, spreading the heavy blue plastic tarp over the pile of uncut wood. When I was finished, I stood for a moment on the flagstone patio, savoring the mingled smells of cedar, damp earth, and the sea. In front of me, a little gravel path wound through a rock garden, and just beyond, over a six-foot drop to a shingle beach, was the ocean. The Pacific. Well, the Strait of Juan de Fuca, at least.

Tonia had been able to move here to this little house by the sea following the sale of her ritzy condo in Uplands. It was a move I heartily applauded — I'd always wanted to know someone with the sea for her back yard. The mortgage on this place must have been really something — none of these cute little places by the sea went for less than two hundred thousand nowadays — but the Uplands condo had helped a lot, I guessed. And Tonia wasn't exactly a pauper. A tenured professor in the Women's Studies Department at U Vic, she had a couple of books to her credit and a tidy stock and bond portfolio. She could afford this house on Marine Drive. But just barely. Last winter's heating bill had been enough to send two kids to college, she claimed, so this winter she planned to heat the house completely with wood. Suffice it to say that I made frequent visits in which I bartered my chopping skills for dinner. It was a fair trade: Tonia didn't do wood, and I don't do dinner.

I thought back to what Tonia had said about my being a courage junkie, about needing to go toe to toe with the Forces of Evil. Maybe there was more truth in that than I wanted to admit. I'd had my ribs broken, my hands burned, and my brains nearly blown out in the course of my particular quest — helping people the system couldn't. And it was true — they did tick me off. They just couldn't be straight. I sighed. Was it people in trouble, or was it everyone? Did we all dissemble? Maybe I *did* want to give up. Maybe I just wanted something safer.

Maybe ... oh, to hell with it, I thought and looked out at the frothy sea. What had Matthew Arnold said?

> Listen! you hear the grating roar
> Of pebbles which the waves draw back and fling
> At their return, up the high strand,
> Begin, and cease, and then again begin,
> With tremulous cadence slow, and bring
> The eternal note of sadness in.
> Sophocles long ago
> Heard it on the Aegean and it brought to mind
> The endless ebb and flow of human misery.

Human misery. Sophocles had certainly gotten that right. I shivered. All this talk of quests, and Niall, and what I used to do at the Crown Prosecutor's office had made me maudlin. And maudlin was no frame of mind in which to pay court to the object of one's affection. No indeedy. So I shut off the Matthew Arnold tape which was playing in my mind, squared my shoulders, and resolved to think cheerful thoughts. Or at least utter cheerful words. With a last look at the roiling sea, I turned and walked up the path to the yellow-lighted windows of Tonia's home.

Fogarty, her recently-acquired black Labrador retriever, met me at the patio door with a polite "ruff" of greeting and a minimum of writhing and wagging. A reserved and gracious fellow, he had seemed to sense immediately that I was a cat person and he never pressed his affections upon me. We had a perfectly amiable relationship. Every once in a while I might be persuaded to throw his tennis ball for him, or take him for a walk, but he never showered me with damp and doggy attentions in return. In fact, he never behaved that way toward anyone.

"Do you think he was a cat in his former life?" I asked Tonia after I had shed my wet shoes and sweatshirt, washed up, and poured myself a finger of Scotch.

"A cat? Well now, that's a thought." She was chopping onions at the kitchen sink, and Fogarty and I were in our accustomed places — me on a stool at the end of the counter, he in his doggie bed in the corner. He thumped his tail once to acknowledge that he was following the conversation.

"What's for dinner?" I asked, raising my arms over my head and stretching.

"Nothing fancy. Oyster stew, a salad. I thought we'd take trays into the living room."

The shrill ring of the telephone interrupted her. "Will you get that?" she asked.

I plucked the phone off the wall by the window expecting to be solicited by one of those annoying dinnertime opportunists selling light bulbs or magazine subscriptions. Instead, I heard the rumble of Sandy's voice.

"Sorry to disturb you," he said apologetically. "I'm dead on my feet but Mary insisted I call. There's something that can't wait."

"Oh?" Not wanting to worry Tonia, I tried to keep my voice neutral, but behind me, I heard the sounds of chopping cease.

"I made sure the motel manager has the stuff he bagged up in a safe place — the clothes, a pair of muddy boots. I pulled a few strings and South Van faxed me the police report. It's a marvel of brevity. No joy there. But if you want to pursue things on your own, I suggest you talk to one of the two officers who went out to investigate. Lynne Hadley. Despite what you think of the South Van force, she's pretty good. I talked to her and she'll let you see the report and the pictures. Unofficially, of course."

"Of course. So what can't wait?" I insisted.

"Well, the thing of it is, she's here. I brought her back with me. I couldn't think what else to do with her so I put her in the garage."

Confused, I thought he meant Lynne Hadley. Then, for one crazy, heart-stopping moment, I was sure it was Jonna. My fevered brain supplied a picture of her sitting in Sandy's car in the dark garage, dead eyes staring into the middle distance. Then I got a grip on myself. "What the hell are you talking about, Alexander?"

"The cat. The little girl's cat. It was hiding outside in the bushes. The motel manager identified it."

I couldn't think of a single thing to say.

"Well? What was I to do with it?" he demanded. "Leave it there? In the pouring rain?"

"Jesus, Sandy. And this is what couldn't wait? What do you want me to do about it?"

"Come and fetch it, of course. It's Jory's. I'm sure she misses it."

I groaned. "Give me a break! Oh, all right. But not tonight. Tomorrow. I'll stop by first thing in the morning. In the meantime, give it a bowl of warm milk and a blanket."

"I already have," he informed me. "And a hot bottle. The wee beastie was positively frozen."

"St. Francis of bloody Assisi," I groused. "Tomorrow, Sandy."

"Hmmmf," he said, and hung up.

"That was Sandy," I told Tonia.

"Mmmhmm," she said noncommittally. "Who on earth needs a bowl of warm milk and a blanket?"

"A cat," I said. Then, with a sigh, I decided to come clean. After all, if we were going to live together, as we had discussed, she was likely to hear more bizarre stories than this. "I got propositioned last night."

She raised an eyebrow.

"By a ten-year-old. The daughter of my best friend in high school. I lived with her for two crazy months during my first year of college. Haven't seen her for twenty-two years. I didn't know where she was. Didn't even know she was married. And I certainly didn't know she had a kid. The last time I saw her, we ... quarreled. I threw her out. She called me once, about eleven years ago, just to talk, she said. But we argued then, too." I shook my head and told her the rest. She didn't interrupt.

"The kid says her father killed her mother," I concluded. "South Van went and checked it out. Sandy flew over to have a look. That was him on the phone. Reporting in."

"Jesus, Caitlin," Tonia said, taking a seat at the table.

"Yeah, pretty sordid, isn't it?" I jammed my hands into the pockets of my jeans.

"Sordid? No. Sad, perhaps. Tragic, even. But more women's lives than we dream about may be like Jonna's." She shook her head. "You said the child propositioned you. What did she want?"

I chuckled mirthlessly. "She wants me to find her father."

"Won't the police do that? South Van?"

"Well, they might if they believed the kid. But they don't."

"Why not?"

"No body."

"What?"

"Jonna's body wasn't where the kid said it was. So Sandy and South Van think she's making this all up. No body, no crime."

"What does she say?"

"Jory says she saw her mother lying dead on the floor. But when South Van got there, the motel room was empty."

"Maybe she was mistaken."

"Maybe," I equivocated.

"Why didn't she call 911?" Tonia wondered.

"Jory says she was afraid — when she saw her mom was dead, she cut and ran. Hopped a bus for the ferry."

Tonia shook her head. "Hmmm. That doesn't quite ring true, does it? She could have called 911 from a convenience store. Or the bus station."

"You're starting to sound like Sandy," I groused. "Listen. The kid's back is covered with scars from old beatings. My candidate for the perp is her father. So no wonder she ran. She was afraid he'd get his hands on her again."

"Still," Tonia said thoughtfully, "wouldn't you have called 911 if it were *your* mother lying there?"

"Yeah. I guess I would have."

"This says an awful lot about the child's relationship with her mother, doesn't it?"

I massaged my eyes with the heels of my hands. "Yeah. It does." Hell, maybe Sandy and Tonia were right. Maybe Jory *was* lying. But why?

"How did she end up on your doorstep?"

"Her mother sent her, I guess. Jonna called me the day before. She said she was afraid for her life and begged me to meet her at the seaplane dock. When I showed up the next day there was no Jonna. Only Jory."

"If Sandy doesn't think she's telling the truth, why do you?" Tonia asked slowly.

"Beats me," I told her. "I guess I'd rather believe her than not because the alternative is so ... messy."

"What do you mean?"

"Well, if Jonna is alive, then where the hell is she?"

"A hospital? Wandering around somewhere with a head injury?"

"Maybe. But South Van checked the hospitals."

"I see. So the question is: if she's alive, why hasn't she contacted you. Presumably she would want to know if Jory was all right."

"Presumably."

"So, given the fact that she hasn't contacted you, it's more logical that she's dead."

I sighed. "Which brings us back to the sixty-four-thousand-dollar question."

"Where's the body?"

"Right."

"Well,'" Tonia said reasonably, "the husband must have taken it."

"Jesus! This sounds like the script for a horror movie. Can you see some guy driving around with the body of his dead wife on the seat beside him?"

"That does seem a little bizarre. Maybe he buried her."

"Unlikely. It was pouring rain last night. Not good burying weather."

"Well then, maybe he *is* driving around with Jonna on the seat beside him, but she isn't dead. Maybe she's hurt. Or maybe she's all right but he's preventing her from getting away."

I thought about this for a moment. "Hmmm. Either of those scenarios would fit."

"If Jory is telling the truth."

"Right."

"Tell me about him. The husband."

"Kirk Ratliffe. The same age as Jonna and me — we were seniors in high school together. A good-looking spoiled rotten kid. He had everything — even a few brains. But he spent his senior year drinking and trying to get in all the girls' pants. A real lady-killer."

Tonia winced. "What an awful phrase."

"Isn't it? It tells you volumes."

"But the question is, did the spoiled lady-killer grow up to be the kind of man who could beat his daughter and kill his wife?"

"I don't know. He liked to bully the other kids but he never did much on his own. It was as though he could only be brave when his cronies were around. I mostly felt sorry for him. He seemed so ... empty."

"But spoiled bullies sometimes grow into disappointed, hopeless young men filled with rage."

"True." I sighed. "Yeah, Ratliffe could have beaten Jory. And killed Jonna. They seemed to have a classic love-hate relationship."

"So Jory wants to hire you to see her father brought to justice."

"Not quite," I told her. "She wants me to find the son of a bitch and kill him."

Her eyes registered shock. "Caitlin, she can't be serious!"

"Like hell. She has five one-hundred-dollar bills that say how serious she is."

"Where is she now?" Tonia asked in a small voice.

"She's at Maggie's. I owe her the courtesy of a reply to her offer."

"You're not seriously considering it!"

"Well, not the killing part of it," I told her. "But she did make me a business proposition. And finding her father, well, that *is* the sort of thing I do. Hell, someone needs to find out what happened in that motel room."

She was quiet for a moment, evidently surprised by the fact that I would consider working for a ten-year-old. Hell, it surprised me, too. Hadn't I decided last night that I wasn't going to have anything to do with this homicidal munchkin? But if I didn't find her father, who would?

"The child's mother. Your friend. Was she . . . were you and she . . ."

"Yeah. We were. Sort of."

"Oh." Silence again. Then, "Do you think you owe her this, Caitlin? Through her child?"

I exhaled heavily. "I don't know, Tonia. I guess that's what she wanted me to think." Well, *did* I owe her? Do we really owe anybody anything? How much claim does your past have on you? I thought of a line from some poem I had read: "We are not now what we were." An eloquent phrase, I had always thought. So why didn't it make dealing with the past any easier?

"Do you still want to stay for supper?" she asked carefully, after another long moment of silence.

I came back to earth. "Of course. Didn't I just work my fingers to the bone out there in the yard?" I grabbed my back dramatically. "My chiropractor will be delighted to see me."

She smiled. "Okay. I'll fix the trays. Will you feed Fogarty?"

Oh goody. Caitlin Reece, the servant of dogs. When he got a whiff of this, Repo would probably use my leg as a scratching post. "Sure."

She got up from the table and came over to put her arms around me. I held her against me and smoothed her glossy hair.

"I'll try," she said.

"Try what?"

"Try not to worry about the small stuff."

"Okay."

"But you have to be honest with me. You have to tell me when I ought to worry. When it's something serious."

I said nothing. Hell, most of the time, even I didn't know the difference.

"I just want to be ... prepared," she said. "Can you understand that?"

"Yes."

"Okay, then." Giving me a quick hug, she went into the dining room.

Fogarty came over to sit at my feet, yellow doggie eyes hopeful.

"C'mon, Foges," I told him, digging in the pantry for his Alpo. "Din din."

"Ruff," he opined.

I couldn't have agreed more.

SUNDAY

Chapter 5

I yawned my way through a shower, dressed in jeans and an ancient pale blue wool turtleneck, tied on my new Brooks sneakers, and pronounced myself ready for the day. A quick peek outside showed me a city wrapped in fog — the kind that didn't look as though it had come on little cat feet. Nor did it seem as though it would burn off anytime soon. With a longing glance at the lump under my blankets that was Repo and Jeoffrey, I steeled myself and made my way out to the kitchen. Just in case they decided to get up sometime today, I dished

71

out food for the two boys, left it on their placemat for them, then took Pansy's into the pantry for her. She had made a comfy little nest in a pile of burlap sacks, and roused sufficiently to give me a slit-eyed look before resuming her slumbers. I felt guilty, though — my pantry was actually an enclosed, unheated back porch.

"What are you, a Spartan?" I asked, kneeling down beside her. "Central heating beckons inside. You can even take your burlap sack." I petted her gently with two fingers and she growled a warning. Prickly Pansy. "Whatever," I said.

I flipped on my Krups coffeemaker and sat down to think about what the hell I was going to do with Jory. There were only so many possibilities.

One, I could send her back to her relatives in the east. Which ones, I wasn't sure. Jonna's family had been poor but big; Kirk Ratliffe's was wealthy and small. Who would take Jory? For that matter, which of them even knew her?

Two, I could pack her off to Social Services. Which brought us back to Option One, except this time it would be faceless strangers who would be sending her back to her relatives.

Three, I could choose to believe her mother was alive, as Tonia had suggested, and set out to find her. Plucking Jonna from the clutches of Kirk Ratliffe, I could reunite mom and daughter and stash them in a safe place while I dealt with dad. Once dad was safely behind bars, mom and daughter would live happily ever after. I poured coffee and snorted. Now there was a fairy tale if I ever heard one.

Four, I could believe that Jory's mother was

dead. That opened up two interesting choices: I could pursue Ratliffe, as Jory wanted me to, or I could wait and let him come for the kid. I didn't doubt he would — according to Jory, he always had.

Well, whatever course of action I decided upon, something had to be done with Jory. She had to stay somewhere, live with someone. She had come to me, so I guessed I was saddled with the problem. But hell, what was I supposed to do with her? Put her in the pantry with Pansy? She was only ten years old — too young to be left alone. And I was gone for most days and often half the nights, too. What did that mean — a babysitter?

I realized with a surge of irritation that I knew absolutely nothing about her — where she had lived, whether she was good in school, what she liked. I knew more about Fogarty than I did about Jory.

I finished the last of my coffee, put my mug in the sink, and walked thoughtfully to the front door. Shrugging my way into my bomber jacket, I wondered if I had what it took to live with a kid, for even a short time. With a *frisson* of dread at the prospect, I closed the door behind me, and I went to fetch my charges.

"She's sick," I told Mary as we bent over the limp form of a skinny, half-grown black cat. Mucus ran from her nose and her breathing could have been heard on the mainland. "She needs to go to the vet. Pronto."

"Thank heavens you agree," Mary said, tucking a wisp of salt-and-pepper hair behind one ear. She pulled her plaid flannel robe a little closer. "Sandy took one look at her this morning, declared it was a 'wee cold,' and told me not to worry."

"This 'wee cold' could be a lot of things. Then again, it could be just that — a cold." I looked around the drafty garage for a cat carrier. "How did he bring her home last night?"

"Just carried her. Stuffed inside his coat."

"Let's make her a nice bed in a cardboard box," I suggested. "How about that one, over there?"

Mary brought over a liquor carton and I gathered up the still form of the little cat, blanket and all, and tried to make a comfy nest without disturbing her too much. She didn't budge. I said goodbye to Mary, loaded the box in my car, and hit the road for Saanich and my friend Emma Neely's veterinary practice.

Forty minutes later, I was banging on Emma's back door, box in hand. In the last few minutes, the cat had begun to gasp for air, and I pounded a little more enthusiastically than I had meant to.

"We're not open till nine," one of Emma's officious little assistants informed me through a window in the door.

"I've got a dying cat and a hundred-dollar bill that says you're open right now," I told her. "Get this door unlocked."

"Oh, it's you," Ginny, Emma's red-haired vet tech, said in dismay. As the result of a previous disagreement regarding Repo, Ginny and I were not on the best of terms.

"Forget about me," I said, shoving the box into her hands. "I'll pay emergency rates for this one. Just start treatment."

She bent to look into the box, then straightened up in alarm. "Allie!" she called to someone in the back, hurrying away with the box. A door slammed and I was left alone.

I tapped my foot for a few moments, but no one appeared. Taking my wallet out of my pocket, I pulled out a hundred, ripped a piece of paper from my notebook, scribbled on it FOR BLACK KITTEN'S CARE, wrapped the hundred in the piece of paper, and thumbtacked it to the door. Someone would be sure to find it there. Then, as there was nothing else I could do here, I trudged on out to my car, prepared to fetch the other abandoned waif that had been placed in my care.

"She's just getting dressed," Maggie told me. "C'mon in. How about breakfast? Robin's going to make French toast."

I wavered, but held firm. "No thanks. I thought I'd take Jory somewhere. So we could talk."

"Good idea," Maggie said, eyeing me curiously. "So?"

"So what?"

"So what are you going to do with her?"

"Damned if I know," I said honestly. "We'll talk. Then I'll decide." I sighed. "Any hints? Our Miss Brooks I'm not."

Maggie poured herself some coffee and leaned against the counter. "She seems pretty tough, but that's probably what she wants us to see. She seems withdrawn, but that's only to be expected given everything she's been through. She's extremely intelligent and more than a little suspicious." Maggie shrugged. "I don't know how helpful that is."

"Me neither. Did she talk? Tell you anything at all?"

"Nothing."

"Did you ask?"

"No."

"Jesus, Maggie!" I lowered my voice. "What am I supposed to *do*? How do you talk to kids, anyhow?"

"Beats me. I never had any. Never wanted to."

Footsteps on the stairs interrupted our unproductive discourse on child management, and Jory came uncertainly into the kitchen. Hair neatly braided, dressed in what was evidently an old red turtleneck and pullover of Robin's, Jory looked well-scrubbed and well-rested. And, I noted with surprise, not at all the cowed, frightened little girl I had met yesterday. Instead, she seemed almost ... poised. Odd, I thought, for someone who's only twenty-four hours away from seeing her mother beaten to death before her eyes. I don't know what I expected, but it wasn't this.

"Caitlin will have to bring you back in a week or so to get those sutures out," Maggie told Jory.

She nodded solemnly. "Thank you," she said to Maggie. Then she turned to me. "Where are we going?"

"To have breakfast," I told her. "Then I thought you might like to come with me while I do a few errands. We might even go shopping. After that, we can go back to my place."

"Okay," she said, face a carefully composed blank mask. She was evidently determined not to give away a thing.

Maggie handed her my parka and she looked at it uncertainly.

"You probably don't need that," I told her. "I'll put the heater on in the car."

"The sun's about to come out," Maggie declared, opening the kitchen curtains. "It's going to be a pretty day. Now go on, you two. I know you have things you need to discuss."

I thought Jory might like the coffee shop at the Oak Bay Marina. It's an unpretentious place and from the windows you can see pleasure craft coming and going, fishing parties returning laden with their catch and, if you're lucky, the local harbor seals.

Jory studied the menu carefully.

"What appeals to you?" I asked.

"Just ... toast, I guess," she said, seeming confused.

I raised an eyebrow. "Just toast? Is that what you usually eat for breakfast? Or are you on a diet?" That got the ghost of a smile from her.

"When Mom and I are ... well, I don't usually eat breakfast," she said, looking embarrassed.

Hell, what she probably meant was they hadn't been able to *afford* breakfast. "Hmmm. Well, pretend it's lunch. Or dinner."

She studied the menu again. "Pancakes," she said finally. "And bacon."

I beckoned the waitress over. "One order of pancakes and bacon, and one Spanish omelette. Sourdough toast, lots of butter. I'll have coffee. Jory?"

Jory looked mystified. I guess she really *didn't* eat breakfast.

"Bring my friend a glass of milk," I told the waitress.

"I just remembered something," Jory said in a low voice, eyes serious. "I didn't bring any *money* with me."

"It's a good thing for us that I did, then," I said, winking at her. "Otherwise we'd have had to do dishes."

"Or sneak out."

Why did I have the feeling that she wasn't joking?

"So," I began, feeling distinctly like an ass. "Tell me a little about yourself. What grade you're in in school. That sort of thing."

She tilted her head and looked at me appraisingly. I bristled. Clearly the kid was sizing me up. "Can I ask you something?" she said.

"Sure. Shoot."

"What I talked to you about last night. Are you going to do it?"

Oh, that. I sighed. "Yes and no."

"What does that mean?"

"Yes, I'll try to find your father." And your mother, too, I vowed silently. Dead or alive. Then, just to make things perfectly clear, I added, "But no, I won't kill him."

She thought this over. "What will you do with him when you find him?"

"I know you don't want me to do this, but I have to," I warned her. "I'll hand him over to the cops."

"What will they charge him with?" she asked, suddenly seeming very much the adult.

Good question. No body, no murder charge. "I don't know the answer to that yet. Possibly murder." She didn't flinch, so I continued. "And this will be different from the other times. This time you have help. There could be other charges, too."

"What other charges?"

"Whatever you're willing to bring against him. You said he hurt people. Did he hurt you, too?"

Her eyes slid away from mine and after a moment's thought, she answered my question with one of her own. "Would they listen to me?"

"Yes, sweetie. They'd listen to you."

"How do you know?" she asked, not challenging me, just asking for information.

"I'm an attorney," I told her. "I used to work in the Crown Prosecutor's office." I wondered how I could make this simple enough for her to understand. "It was my job to prepare cases against the bad guys. To try and get them put in jail. Sometimes children were involved. Usually, they were ... well ..." I trailed off. Hell, I couldn't make this any simpler. She'd just have to get what she could from it. "Usually they were victims. Sometimes they were witnesses. Sometimes they were both."

"Witnesses," she said, considering the word. "Like, they saw what happened?"

"Yeah."

"Oh," she said, digesting all this.

Our breakfasts came, and before I had my sourdough toast buttered, she was well into her pancakes. She cleaned her plate with such rapidity and looked at it so disconsolately that I decided serious measures were called for.

"Want seconds?"

"May I?"

"Sure." I called the waitress over and ordered the same thing again. She looked at us in amusement and went off to place the order.

"So you'll ... do it? Help?" she asked, stumbling over the words.

"Yes. I said so." I finished off my omelette and sat back, sipping my coffee. "And now I'm going to tell you what you have to do." She gave me an I-told-you-so look, but I waved it aside. "This is the speech I give every client. It's not something I made up specially for you. So listen up, Jory."

She shrugged. What choice did she have? "Okay."

"We have to be absolutely straight with each other. You have to answer all my questions honestly, give me all the information I need. No lies, ever. If I ask you a question, it's because I think the answer is important."

She nodded. I noted, however, that her eyes were on the table, not on me. That bothered me, so I reached over and tilted her chin up so our eyes met.

"This is the big leagues, kid. If you lie to me and I catch you at it, I quit."

"Okay." Her voice was a husky whisper.

"I'm going to treat you like an adult. Just like my other clients. No coddling."

She nodded and I patted her cheek.

"That means you have to do what I tell you. Even if you don't understand my reasons. You'll just have to believe that I know what I'm doing." I skewered her with my toughest look. "Well?"

"What about you?" she asked.

"What about me?"

"Well, will *you* lie? You know, tell a fib because

I'm a kid and you think you need to protect me or something?"

That was a damned good question. "No," I said, making up my mind abruptly. "I won't. You're paying full fare, so you get the full ride. Right to the end of the line."

"You promise?"

"Yeah, I promise."

That should have reassured her but suddenly she felt the need to twirl one of her braids around a finger. At the same time, her left foot began a drum tattoo against the restaurant bench. Her eyes glazed over and she studied her empty plate as if it were the Rosette Stone.

"What's on your mind, Jory?" I asked quietly.

"I ... he ..." she lifted her eyes from her plate and gave me a gaze full of misery.

I sighed. This was going to be tough. "You're afraid of him. Right?"

Nodding, she twirled her braid faster.

"Jory, tell me the worst thing that could happen."

That stopped her twirling. "He'd come and get me," she said in a voice about six years younger than her usual belligerent croak. "He'd take me away, like he always said he would. 'Jory, we'll go and live in Heaven,' he'd say. 'Just the two of us.' But I don't want to go with him!"

There was something wrong here, but I let it pass because I sensed she was about to tell me something important. And because I felt a little sick about what I thought she was going to tell me.

Her eyes got very red and I realized she was trying hard not to cry. "I never told anyone," she said. "Not Mom or Grandma Ratliffe or anyone."

"Why not, Jory?"

"I ... I didn't think they'd believe me," she said miserably, winning the battle against her tears. "Sometimes, well, sometimes I make things up. You know, stories. About dragons and witches. Once I made up one about a UFO."

"Stories? You mean you write them?"

She squirmed. "Sometimes. Other times, well, I kind of live in them."

"You live in them?"

"Yeah. Like, there was one month I was on a sacred journey and I called Mr. Andresson Mordred, and Mrs. Andresson was Nimue. They work for Grandma," she explained.

"Who were you?"

"Parsifal."

"Hmmm. What did the Andressons think?"

"They thought I was odd." She looked troubled at that. "I *am* odd — I know that. They were patient, though," she said with an adult's charity.

"Hmmm. Making things up can be inconvenient if you want to be believed for something that's real but sounds far-fetched."

"Yeah."

"So, you make things up and you think that's why no one will believe you about your father."

"Yeah."

Well, the kid had a point. No wonder she'd wanted to know if anyone would believe her were she to testify against her father. And already the deck was stacked against her — both Sandy and South Van were not impressed with her veracity. I wondered how to change that. Find Jonna's body, I thought grimly.

"Jory, I need to tell you something."

She looked at me in alarm. "It's something bad, isn't it?"

Ah shit. But how could I make it any easier for her? "It might be. And then again it might not be. But I need you to think about it real hard."

She nodded, eyes wary.

"When the police went to investigate at the motel last night, they didn't find your mother."

I don't know what I expected, but whatever I did, I didn't get it. She registered absolutely no emotion at all. Instead, she said rather primly, "You mean they didn't find her body."

"Well, yes."

"So they think I made up a story about him killing her," she said calmly.

"Yes, they do," I said, amazed at her total lack of emotion.

"Do you think I made up a story?"

Jesus — did I? I thought about what I had promised her, about not fibbing. Because I was tempted to. *Yes, Jory, I believe you absolutely.* But that would have been bigger than a fib; it would have been one monstrous whopper. The last half hour had shown me a scary, and perhaps disturbed, human being, ten years old or not. "Let's just say that there could be several interpretations of the facts."

"What does that mean?"

"It means that when South Van didn't find your mother's body they jumped to the obvious conclusion — that you were making it up."

She said nothing, eyes on my face, waiting.

"There are at least three other ways to look at it.

One, your father moved the body. Two, your father moved what you *thought* was your mother's body —"

"I —"

I held up a hand to cut off her objection. "Let me finish. Then you can have your turn. This is the big times, junior. We have a problem here and one way or another we have to work it out. You're not a trained professional." She sulked, but I ignored it. "Neither am I. Sometimes folks who look pretty dead one minute can get up the next and scare the pants off you. I know this from experience. Option three is that your mother got up and moved herself." And of course Option four is that Jory made it up, I told myself bleakly.

She had stopped sulking and resumed braid-twirling. I was almost sure she hadn't heard a word I said when she rasped; "I just thought of number four."

Trying to keep my thoughts off my face, I repeated, "Number four?"

"Yeah. What if Mom wasn't dead at all? What if I was wrong like you said and she woke up and went with him because she wanted to?"

Oh goody. Now there was a happy prospect. A little domestic rough stuff, a little kissy-face, then business as usual. It was as credible as the other three scenarios except for one thing. Jonna's frantic phone call to me, and Jory's presence. Still, it was worth exploring.

"Did they often behave like that?"

"Like what?" she asked, playing dumb.

I groaned. "Jory, I know this is hard —"

"Okay, yes," she hissed. "Yes! He hit her a lot. And he hit me too when he could get his hands on me. But she ... she ..." Her eyes got red again and this time she lost the fight with her tears. "She always told him where we were when he got out of prison. Always." Angrily, she dashed the tears from her eyes with one sleeve. "Then he'd come and get us, and they'd start drinking again and pretty soon he was hitting her and doing bad stuff and then he'd be in jail again." She blew her nose on her napkin and fell silent.

"What did you and your mom do when he, when your father was in jail?"

She shrugged. "I don't know what she did. She'd send me to Grandma Ratliffe's for a while. Then, after a few months she'd come and get me and we'd just ... drive places."

"Drive places?"

"Yeah, like we were getting away. She always seemed so scared."

I thought I understood. "But you never did get away, did you?"

She looked at me once then hung her head in what I took for shame. "No," she said, fists clenched. "Why couldn't she have just left me at Grandma Ratliffe's?" she asked me. "Why did she have to drag me along, too? They didn't want me there. When they got together all they did was drink and watch TV and fight."

"I don't know what to say, Jory. Sometimes women behave that way with men who beat them. And their children," I added.

Fury and contempt were plain in her eyes. "Why? Why do they do it?"

I shrugged. How could I make this phenomenon easy to understand when wiser heads than mine didn't understand it? "I don't know, sweetie," I said. "Mostly they're confused. About what love is, and about what they owe themselves."

"And their kids," she said huskily.

"Yeah. And their kids." I was surprised at the undercurrent of disgust in her voice and for the first time I realized that she might well have as much reason to hate Jonna as she did to hate Kirk. After all, it was Jonna who had failed to keep her safe, who had delivered her time after time into the hands of the monster. A monster who may well have stopped beating her only when he discovered another use for her.

"Did you have a special friend?" I asked, hoping it was so, my heart breaking for her.

"Just La Belle," she said.

"Who was that?"

"Grandma Ratliffe's cat." Her voice brightened a little. "I took one of her kittens, News, with me when we ... when my mom and I ran away last month. But *he* threw it out the window after he found us. He called it Bad News. He was always throwing it around or kicking at it. When I tried to stop him, he pushed me and I fell against the dresser."

"That's when you cut your head," I guessed.

She said nothing, her mind clearly on News. I wondered if I should tell her that it was now at Emma Neely's. Probably not. After all, we didn't know if it would live.

"Where did your mom stay when she sent you to your grandma's?"

"With her people. On the reservation." She looked

up at me with that expressionless gaze again. "The Ratliffes were too rich for her, she said."

"Did you ever live with your mom?" I asked.

"Yeah. Until I was five. He was in prison then, in Kingston. Once he got out, though, all the trouble started."

"Where did you live when you ran away?"

She shrugged her skinny shoulders. "In awful places — motels, deserted houses, in our car, with some of Mom's friends. If it was summer, we camped."

"When you ... what did your grandma think of you and your mom traipsing all over the country?" I was surprised that the old lady hadn't contacted Child Protective Services and gotten custody. The Viola Ratliffe I had known was one hell of a tough cookie.

Jory considered this. "She said it was ridiculous. She said the two of them were going to be the death of each other and that they should just go off somewhere and settle things. She didn't take my mom's side," Jory explained matter-of-factly. "She told them they should leave me out of it."

I shook my head. A very sordid picture was emerging — one which didn't go very far towards painting Jonna as a helpless victim. And when I thought about it, I realized it might well be accurate. Ratliffe had held a fascination for Jonna when we were young, as had she for him. Their behavior as adults had simply grown out of their relationship as adolescents. But Jory ... Her grandmother was right. She should have been left out of it. Why the hell did Jonna drag her along time after time? It was particularly incomprehensible given the fact that Jonna always broke down and let the son of a bitch know where they were. I shook my head. This didn't add up. I was in over my head and decided I'd have to ask for elucidation from someone who knew more about this than I did. But that would have to be later. Right now there were a few more questions I wanted to ask Jory.

"You said your ... Kirk had been in jail several times. What for?"

She shrugged. "He drank a lot. He never had any money. So he'd get mad and break things. He stole things, made my mom and me steal them, too. Once he stole a car, but he was too drunk to drive and crashed it into a store. That's how the police caught him. He would do these things after he'd been living with us for a while."

I shook my head. This was worse than horrible.

Jory twirled her braid again. "Why didn't my mom ask you for help before now?"

I took a deep breath. "The last time I saw her we had an argument. We never patched it up. That was, oh, twenty-two years ago."

"You mean you didn't talk to her for twenty-two years?"

"Right."

"So you didn't even *know* about me?"

"Not until yesterday."

"But you knew about Guy, right?"

"Guy?"

"My brother. Guy. He died when he was two. That was a long time before I was born."

I felt something turn over in my heart. "How long?"

She wrinkled her brow. "Eleven years, I think. There was something wrong with him," Jory told me. He was . . ." She frowned, trying to remember the word. "He was autistic. Grandma said he would never have been right. He stayed at a place in the country with other people like him. Grandma paid for it."

I was long past amazement.

"What did you and Mom argue about?" Jory wanted to know.

I guessed she deserved to know. "Your father."

She looked at me skeptically. "Were you both in love with him?"

The idea was so absurd that I laughed out loud. "No, nothing like that."

"Well?"

"I didn't think your mom ought to . . . have anything to do with him," I said carefully, trying to keep my voice steady, to encompass Jonna's betrayal of me in nice, neutral words, to keep any shred of pain buried deep. "I knew she was thinking of . . . marrying him, and I didn't think he would treat her very well, Jory."

Her eyes were unreadable. "Well, you were right," she said in her husky croak. She withdrew into herself then, and for many long moments, I just watched her. This was what The Jonna and Kirk Story had produced — a child who could shut off her emotions at will, whose contempt for her mother was almost palpable, and who could hire a total stranger to murder her father. A child of violence.

"How much will finding him cost?" she asked at last.

I took a deep breath, happy to deal with the

present. "Okay, let's talk about money. What I usually do is this. My clients pay me a retainer and when the job is over, I bill them for the rest. I charge two-fifty a day plus expenses."

"Okay," she said.

"I don't know how long this is likely to take, Jory. It depends on where he's gone, and how well he's covered his tracks. But let's not worry about money."

"I have four hundred dollars more."

"So, I'd better find him soon," I said jokingly. "Otherwise, you'll be broke."

She gave me that deadpan, cold-as-ice look and I shivered. "Yes, you'd better," she said.

Why did I get the feeling that *she* wasn't joking. "Well," I said brightly. "Want to go shopping?"

"Shopping?"

"Yeah. You know, buying things. Charging them on the old credit card."

"But I —"

"Oh, heck, we'll send Grandma Ratliffe the bills," I said. "She'd want you to have more than the clothes you arrived in."

"We-ell," she said, making two syllables of it. "All right."

"Great," I said, throwing a handful of bills down on the table. "I have a few errands to do." I was looking forward to thinking things over while Jory was trying on clothes. Jesus. What I didn't know about this case could make a mini-series.

Chapter 6

It was well after noon when we got back to my place — a black and white Tudor-style duplex on Monterey Street, in the heart of Oak Bay. The day had turned grim and windy while we'd driven around shopping and doing my errands, but Jory seemed as happy as a tick. Whenever I had to stop to make a pickup or a delivery, she just pulled out a book and buried her nose in it.

While we were on Government Street, buying a couple of sweaters, Jory had spotted Monroe's Books. After a few moments of dithering, she'd bought the entire collection of *The Chronicles of Narnia,* declaring that Grandma Ratliffe would think this was okay.

Now, after stops at Lester's photo shop, the post office, and the bank, we were back at my house. While Jory was busy in the guest bedroom unpacking purchases, I sat down to make a few quick phone calls.

The first was to Emma Neely's clinic. Guiltily, I realized I'd forgotten about the damned cat until I'd walked in the door and seen my own faithful duo.

"It's Caitlin Reece," I told the young woman who answered the phone. "How's the black kitten I brought in earlier today?"

"Very ill." I recognized Ginny's voice and ground my teeth. "It ought to have had treatment days ago," she said accusingly. I felt my blood pressure rise about twenty points. "Please hold," she said in dismissal.

"Caitlin!" a hearty voice said after only a few moments of Muzak.

"Emma! For God's sake, haven't you explained to your staff that I'm not Attila the Hun? Just because I couldn't diagnose Repo's depression last year doesn't mean I'm not a caring and responsible pet owner. And that black thing isn't even mine!"

"Oh, that's just Ginny," Emma said, pooh-poohing my ire. "She overreacts. Ignore her. She's one helluva good tech."

"Well, her client rapport is nil," I insisted. "If that kid's going to make it as a vet, she's going to need her attitude adjusted."

Emma ignored me. "Okay. Black kitten, let's see. It's got ear mites and fleas, and a dandy upper respiratory infection. It's leukemia negative — there's some good news. If it's still alive tomorrow, it'll probably make it. Want to call back then?"

Crap. Just what I needed — a sick cat who required medicating every couple of hours. "Okay," I said, resigned, and hung up.

I had Sandy on my mind, and when the phone rang, I half expected it to be he. Instead, an unfamiliar male voice growled, "Caitlin Reece?"

"Yeah. Who wants her?"

"This is Kirk Ratliffe. I think you'll remember me."

Arrogant sonofabitch. "Kirk Ratliffe, Kirk Ratliffe . . ." I said thoughtfully. "Didn't you fix my car last month?"

"Oh come off it," a wary voice answered. "You know who this is. Give me my kid," he said.

My heart began a drum solo and almost automatically I hit the CONV button on my answering machine. I wanted this on tape!

"Listen, don't play games with me," he warned, voice pitched low. Was there someone close by he didn't want to hear? Who? My heart gave a leap — Jonna?

"Okay, we won't play games. South Van police want you for murder one," I invented. "How's that?"

"Murder one? Oh yeah? Who am I supposed to have murdered?"

"Your wife, you dumb shit!" I yelled.

"Says who?"

"The witness you left behind. Your daughter."

He gave a little nervous laugh. "Is that what she said. She always was a liar. Christ, Jonna would have been better off to have strangled her as soon

93

as she was born. But that's not your business. It's mine. And Jonna's. I know she's gone running to you to try and get you on her side. But I'm hoping you're smarter than that," he said silkily.

"I'm smart enough not to give her back to you."

"I'm not going to hurt her. I'm her *father* for chrissake!" It was the first emotional outburst he had had, and I thought if only I could provoke him to a few more he might reveal something.

"I know," I said sweetly. "And that's what makes it so disgusting."

"Jesus," he said heatedly. "You women stick together, don't you? Like a bunch of damned hens. And you're about as smart as a bunch of hens, too. Don't you know when you're being played for a sucker, Reece. Jory is, well, she's got a problem. Always has had."

Jesus, here was someone else telling me the kid was lying. "What problem?"

"She doesn't know what's real and what isn't. She lives in some kind of fairy tale. It's all my damned mother's fault, letting her read those books. Jory always was able to wrap her around her little finger. And now she's got you, too."

"That may be," I told him, "but let's not forget that your wife sent Jory to me. No one imagined that."

"Listen, Jonna didn't *send* her to you," he said evenly. "She just went. Oh, I know Jonna called you for help. She was a little excited. Hell, we play rough with each other — that's no secret. But she didn't *send* Jory to you. That was the kid's idea."

"I don't believe you."

"I don't care what you fucking believe," he said,

finally losing it. "But that kid isn't yours. She belongs to me. What happens to her is none of your business."

"Maybe. Maybe not. Tell me what happened in that motel room, Kirk. Tell me what happened to Jonna."

"That's none of your business, either!" he yelled. "That's a family matter. And no matter what happens, we're a family. That's something you could never understand, you dumb dyke."

That's when *I* lost it. "Oh yeah? We'll just see who's dumb here!" I yelled back. "You beat your wife to death and now you want to get your hands on your daughter? Well, you're not having her, and that's the end of it."

"No, that's not the end of it! I'll just come and get her. She belongs to me, not you. I want her. So don't get in my way."

I couldn't help myself. "Oh yeah? Nothing will give me greater pleasure than to get in your way. You'll have to come through me to get Jory, and you'll never do that, Ratliffe. Never. Because you're not half smart enough to figure out how, asshole." I slammed the receiver down. What the hell, I had nothing to lose by terminating the conversation. There was nothing useful on the tape, no clues as to where the hell he was.

The phone rang again. I took the receiver off and forced myself to walk away.

"Caitlin?" a voice whispered from the hallway. "Was that . . . him?"

Oh shit. I'd forgotten all about her. "Jory," I said, holding out a hand to her, "come here." To my relief, she came. I put my arms around her and pulled her close. "Yeah, that was him," I said, holding her tight.

"I heard what you told him," Jory said, a quaver in her voice. "Can you really do it?"

"Sure I can," I said with much more confidence than I felt. I hunkered down beside her. "I haven't lost a client yet." She smiled a little tremulously. "I want to take you someplace safe. Someplace he doesn't know about and can never, never find. Is that all right with you?"

"Will you be there too?"

"Some of the time. Most of the time I'll be looking for him, though."

Poor kid. What could she say. "Okay," she agreed.

"There's a big suitcase in the cupboard in your room," I told her, squeezing her shoulder. "Put your new clothes in it. Your books, too."

"Where I'm going ... do they like kids?"

I knew what she was asking me. She wanted to know if she'd be safe from men like her father. A fair question. I thought of what I could say to reassure her. "In the books you like to read, the ones about dragons and princes and magic, do you remember the good witches, the ones who use white magic to help people? The ones who can talk to animals?"

"Sure."

"Well, we're going to see a good witch."

"Caitlin, those are only stories," she told me, her voice indulgent. "There are no witches. Everyone knows that." But her eyes told me that she wanted to believe something else.

"Oh no?" I said, standing up and walking her to the bedroom. "Tell that to my friend. Her name is Gray Ng. She's from Vietnam and she lost her job because she *is* a witch. And she really can talk to animals."

She tilted her head to look up at me, half-charmed, half-doubtful. "Really?"

I huffed a little for effect. "Really. Remember our bargain? No lies. Not even fibs."

Still skeptical, she hurried off to pack.

Jory was silent on the drive to Gray's. To tell the truth, I was happy not to have to make conversation. There was something decidedly rotten in the state of Denmark, and I wasn't quite sure what. I did, though, have a dandy bunch of choices. Either I believed Jory or I believed Kirk Ratliffe. Either I believed Jory or I believed Sandy and South Van. Either I believed Jonna was dead or I believed she was alive. Either I believed Jory was an innocent witness to her mother's death or I believed she was capable of a monstrous lie. But a lie for what purpose? Try though I might, I couldn't find a motive. But, a little imp of doubt whispered to me, Ratliffe had been pretty convincing on the phone. And where in hell was Jonna's body? Shit. I closed my eyes for a moment, longing for a couple of aspirin and a slug of hot coffee. I felt depressed, anxious, and downright mean.

Right now, however, I had another pair of choices confronting me: either I waited for Ratliffe to come to me, or I went to him. I knew which course of action I preferred, but would I be able to piece together enough facts to formulate a plan of action? After all, if I was going to go get him, I had to know where in hell he was. I drummed my fingers on the wheel in frustration.

Seemingly on autopilot, my MG turned off the Saanich Highway onto the little wooded lane that led to Gray's property. The alders that line the road had long ago lost their leaves and now they stood like an army of the dead — spindly gray-splotched arms reaching up to beg a kinder fate from heaven.

Here at the northern tip of the Saanich peninsula, twenty miles outside Victoria, the land slopes to the sea, and as we drove down the lane to Gray's, we could catch an occasional silver glint from the ocean. In fact, Gray owned a fifteen-acre parcel between the highway and the ocean, but it was so dense with alders, firs, Gary oaks, and arbutus that only in the winter could anyone tell that the ocean lay barely a couple of hundred yards behind her house.

The lane opened up to a small meadow ringed with cedars, and right in the center of the meadow was a cedar-shingled geodesic dome which housed Gray's home and animal psychology practice. This afternoon Gray was in the yard, digging in one of the flowerbeds, black pants tucked into rubber boots, a tan down vest worn unzipped over a black sweatshirt. Her constant companions, a pair of enormous brindled Great Danes she called The Girls, roused at the sound of my car and came loping over to investigate. I parked on the gravel apron at the side of the dome, then rolled down my window so The Girls could get a whiff of me. I held out a hand and The Girls whuffed over it a little, then hurried back to Gray to make their report. She patted them, stuck her shovel in the flowerbed, and came over to the car.

"Good afternoon, Caitlin," she said as I got out of the car. "Your arrival is well-timed. I was just about to make tea."

"Um, I have a favor to ask you," I started.

She put her hands in the pockets of her vest and looked up at me, her almond-shaped eyes holding mine. I hate it when she does that — I imagine she's reading my mind. And maybe she is. "The answer is yes, of course," she said, a small smile on her lips.

A wind from the sea ruffled her short-cropped hair — a small, slender woman of indeterminate age, from a culture so different from mine that I could only guess at her upbringing. She was one of the few people in this world that I admired and respected. Why? She was ... complete.

"I haven't told you what it is yet," I protested.

"Of course you have," she chided gently. "Tell the young lady to take her belongings inside. You may show her to the loft." She closed her eyes and breathed deeply. "There will be a storm tonight. I must make sure the bay pony is comfortable in the barn. You may start tea," she called to me as she walked away. The Girls padded obediently after her.

"C'mon, Jory," I said, opening the car door. "Let's take your stuff inside."

"Was that her?" Jory wanted to know, seeming a

little disappointed. After all, I had promised her a witch.

"Yup. That's her."

"Is it ... all right that we're here?"

"I didn't even have to ask," I told her truthfully.

"You mean, she knew we were coming?"

"Something like that."

"Wow," Jory said as she dragged her suitcase out of the back of my car.

We were all in the back of Gray's house, in the large room she uses for her practice. It has several walk-in cages and today one of them was occupied by a fine-boned, elegant short-haired tortoiseshell cat.

"She bites," Gray warned when Jory wanted to go in and visit her.

"Oh." Jory sounded wistful. "So I can't see her?"

"Certainly you may," Gray said. "When you stroke her, she will bite you, though, and it will hurt. Are you afraid?"

"I don't want to be bitten, but I'm not exactly afraid," Jory said. Then, "Why does she bite?"

"Ah," Gray said. "That, of course, is the question."

"Oh."

Gray smiled. "Do not pull away when she bites. And do not cry out. Instead, leave your hand in her mouth and send her a strong picture of your disappointment. If you send her the right picture, she will let you go."

"What if she doesn't?"

"Then she has not received the picture. You must try again."

"Okay," Jory said seriously. "What's her name?"

"Brandy."

Jory wrinkled her nose. "That's a dumb name for a cat."

"I agree. Perhaps she will tell you her real name."

"Like in *Old Possum's Book of Practical Cats*," Jory said, eyes alight. "Her third name. Her *secret* name."

"Just so."

"Hi, Brandy," Jory said confidently, opening the cage and joining Brandy in her well-clawed armchair. "We're going to be friends."

I wasn't so sure, but we left them together to discuss it.

"Thanks," I said to Gray as she poured tea. We sat in her snug library, a fire crackling in the woodstove, the afternoon ebbing away to evening outside her windows. On the raised brick hearth, one of The Girls snoozed. The other had remained with Jory, no doubt to supervise the biting session. "So how *did* you know what I wanted?" I asked curiously. "You said yes before I ever asked you a thing."

Unhurriedly, Gray sipped tea from a glazed clay cup, cradling it in her palms. She returned it carefully to the table beside her and tucked her feet up under herself. "The large suitcase in the boot of your car spoke to me quite eloquently. And consider this: do you think you brought this sad, maimed child to me by accident? I do not run a hotel. You could have boarded her anywhere. Yet you chose to bring her here."

I thought this over. Was Gray right? Had I chosen to bring Jory here, knowing that Gray was a healer of broken creatures? I shivered. Maybe Shakespeare had been right after all. "There are more things in heaven and earth, Horatio, than are dreamt of in your philosophy," Hamlet had said, chiding his dull friend. Perhaps that was how Gray thought of me: the quintessential left-brained clod.

"There are no accidents," she said quietly. "Only choices. I am flattered that you chose me. I will do what I can. Now, tell me the child's story."

I did, and when I was through, Gray sat back, looking out the window into the night. Whatever she thought or felt, she was keeping it to herself. "I can keep Jory safe from her father," Gray said at length. "But who will keep you safe?"

I bristled. This was the third person in as many days who had suggested that I might need help. First Sandy, then Emma Neely, and now Gray. What was going on? Was I giving off wimpy vibes? "Keeping myself safe is up to me," I told her a little acerbically. "If I can't do that, hell, what can I do?"

She smiled. "I am not referring to your body," she said. Reaching over, she took my right hand in hers and folded the fingers into a fist. "You are strong and competent. You place yourself like a rock in the path of evil." Then she began to unfold my fingers. "I am referring to the spirit. Because it is invisible, some might assume it does not exist." She held my hand, palm up. "What do you see?"

"Nothing," I told her honestly. "An empty hand."

"It is all in how you look," she said. "I see something else. I see inside to the essence of your strength, your determination. I see the tiger's heart. And that is what your strength must preserve, like an oyster protecting its pearl. I see your spirit. Your soul."

I shivered again, believing what I had half-jokingly told Jory. This woman *was* a witch. Anyone who thought that she was just an eccentric little Vietnamese emigre with a strange profession saw very little. It was just as Gray had said: it is all in how you look.

"Protect yourself," she told me. "Close around your spirit, your tiger's heart, like an oyster, like a fist, like a mother. It is your greatest treasure. You must guard it more carefully than you do your life."

I was embarrassed and, as I usually do at such times, I sought refuge in humor. "Like a cat's third name?"

"For a white man of European descent, Mr. Eliot showed flashes of rare understanding," she said, smiling. "As do you, sometimes. Yes, exactly like a cat's third name." Her smile faded. "Take care, Caitlin."

Uncomfortable under the gaze of her dark, dark eyes, I said nothing.

"Gray," I said, starting to ask her about the contradiction posed by Jory's and her father's versions of the truth, to ask for insight. But Jory interrupted me.

"She didn't bite me," she said triumphantly, coming into the room with the second of The Girls at her side.

"Well done," Gray told her. "Sit over here. Would you like some tea?"

"Yes, thank you," Jory said, displaying manners that would have made Grandma Ratliffe beam. I looked at her dispassionately, trying to subtract emotion from my assessment. Could she be lying? Of course she could be, I admitted wearily. Everyone, alas, is capable of it.

"Perhaps I'll leave you two together," I said, getting up. "You can discuss feline management." I looked down at Jory. "You'll be safe here with Gray. I'll check in with you daily. Don't worry. We'll get him."

She gave me a brave little smile. I let myself out before she asked me how.

My house was cold, dark, and empty so I built a fire, turned on all the lights, put on a tape of *The Brandenburg Concertos,* and called my cats. Repo and Jeoffrey appeared from behind the armchair, blinking and stretching, and I hugged them hello, brought them a treat of smoked salmon, and left them stretched out on the rug in front of the fireplace. That left me with the problem of dinner. And Tonia. I called her.

"It's me," I told her, kicking off my shoes and pouring a splash of Scotch into a tumbler. "Caitlin. Your errant woodchopper."

"Errant is right," she said. "I expected you hours

ago. Fogarty and I have already eaten the salmon casserole," she said meaningfully.

"I got a phone call from Jory's dad," I explained. "Apparently he's hot on her trail. So I stashed her at Gray's. I decided to play sitting duck alone."

"Caitlin!" Tonia exploded. "How can you be so cavalier? There's a maniac coming for you and all you can do is wisecrack."

"What do you want me to do?" I asked testily. "Weep? Gibber? Beat my breast?"

"I don't know," Tonia said wearily. "I just think you ought to be ... more careful. Shouldn't you tell Sandy? Ask for police protection?"

"Of course I won't tell Sandy. He doesn't think there's a case here anyhow. No, I have some ideas of my own. And besides a couple of cops sitting out front would just be in the way." I took a deep breath, wondering how to say the next line. "Tonia, I don't want to see you until this thing's over."

"What?" she said. "Why not?"

"Think about it," I said. "If Ratliffe really is out there, and I have no reason to believe he isn't, I'll just draw him to you. I won't do that."

I heard her exhale sharply. I didn't say a word. This was a tense time in our relationship and I didn't want to make things worse. Apart from my reservations about how Fogarty, Repo, Jeoffrey, and Pansy would hit it off, I wasn't at all convinced that I wanted to live with *anyone*, let alone Tonia. In my experience (limited but nonetheless valid) the myth of domestic bliss is just that — a myth. I think it's another one of the scripts men have written to make their lives easier and to keep women under their thumbs, and I don't quite see how it can be adapted so sane people can make use of it. But maybe it ought not to be adapted. Maybe it ought to be scrapped. There are plenty of other living arrangements that seem to me to have greater potential for success than the Let's-Get-Married-And-Mingle-Our-Assets arrangement. That particular scenario is, in my opinion, far too reminiscent of the heterosexual model whence it sprang, and its ready-made roles and expectations. The whole thing was a minefield I had no intention of crossing.

A frosty note crept into her voice. "I'm sure you know what's best."

Shit. "Come off it, Tonia, this is common sense. The last thing I want is to get a phone call from Ratliffe offering to trade me you for Jory. I don't understand your problem with this."

"Call me when you're free," she said.

"Yeah, I will."

And that was that.

The house loomed around me: too many dark corners and hiding places. I finished my Scotch, stared moodily at the fire for a while, and decided that I could feel like prey or I could feel like a predator. I much preferred the latter.

Picking up the phone, I dialed a number you will never find in any directory. Frances the Ferret answered on the fourth ring.

"A Christmas vacation in Maui," he squealed, when I told him what I needed. "That sounds just ducky."

"Ducky, my ass," I growled. "I need this information and I need it fast. Can you get it?"

"Can I?" He was plainly insulted. Francis claimed that there was no piece of information anywhere that, once committed to a database, was safe from his electronic prying. So far he had made good on his claim.

"Pardon me, maestro," I told him. "If I seem a little prickly, it's because the sonofabitch threatened my life a few hours ago. So I'm just a trifle edgy."

"You're entitled," he said magnanimously. "Take five deep breaths — I won't even charge for them — then tell me exactly what you need."

Instead, I counted to ten. "His name's Kirk Ratliffe. Home town, Ottawa. I knew him when I was a kid. He's forty-two. His birthday's March 20. He's been in and out of jail — in Ontario, I assume. I want to know where and what for. Yesterday odds are he beat his wife to death in a motel near the ferry. South Van will have his file by now. I want it. He comes from a wealthy family back east. I want to know what he's doing in B.C. I seem to recall that the family has property here. I want to know what and where."

"No problemo," he assured me.

"Listen, Francis. This guy thinks I have something he wants. He's coming to get it and has warned me not to get in his way. He may have already killed his wife so I don't have to belong to Mensa to figure out that getting rid of me will be like swatting a fly to him. He just doesn't give a shit. I need an edge. I need to know *now* where he's holed up. He's got a base somewhere. He's buying food, maybe clothes and booze and other things. He undoubtedly has a car. Is he buying gas? Is he using credit cards? Hell, no one uses cash anymore. He's got to have left a trail. Let's pick it up."

"For you I'll be especially creative," Francis cooed.

I didn't rise to the bait. "How much?" I asked him wearily.

"The usual. Five crisp hundreds at my mail drop first thing in the morning. But because you're such a good customer, I'll get started on it tonight."

What a guy. "You're all heart," I told the little leech.

"I am, aren't I?" he agreed. "Merry Christmas, sweetie."

That done, I poured a little more Scotch and went in search of supper. There was one ice-covered box of Lean Cuisine vegetable lasagna in my freezer and I eyed it with distaste. Since Tonia had been cooking for me, I had lost my enthusiasm for microwave dinners. *Tough luck, kid,* I told myself, tossing the box in the sink and attacking it with a knife. What would Gray say? Something Confucian like "When romance fails, try technology." That sounded so good that I said it aloud, but it didn't change the fact that I felt depressed, anxious, and very much alone. *To hell with it,* I thought, tossing the lasagna in the microwave and turning the Bach up a few notches. I was damned if I was going to sit and feel sorry for myself.

"Lester, my boy," I said, dialing a number that, unlike the Ferret's, is in the B.C. Tel directory.

"I have those pictures from your last job," he told me, evidently surprised that I'd called him at home. "You can come by for them tomorrow. Er, that is, unless you need them tonight. I guess I could bring them over."

"No, tomorrow is fine. I called you for something else. Remember that surveillance job I did a few weeks back?"

"Sure. You wanted me to install hidden video cameras but we couldn't get in in time to do it. So I gave you some equipment and you took pictures from outside. Why? Do you want video surveillance someplace else?"

"Yeah. My place."

"Oh." I could hear him swallow. Poor Lester. He just isn't cut out for a life of crime. He's exactly what he seems to be — a polite, clean-cut, conservative Canadian youth. Well, he *did* inherit his employer's thriving photography business last year at the tender age of twenty-two, but in all other respects he was pretty typical. In my mind's eye, I could see him in the apartment (also inherited) over the photo shop, fussing around making dinner — a lanky, sandy-haired, blue-eyed kid with aviator glasses, dressed in a button-down shirt, crisply pressed khaki pants, white socks, and Topsiders. He was the kind of guy any mother would be proud to have as a son-in-law: a nice guy. And he cooked, too.

In the past several months, Lester had begun to diversify the photo shop business. Now Henderson's Photos carried several lines of expensive video cameras and recorders, and Lester had plans to convert the property's sizeable garage into a videotape rental business. What the heck — he had the capital to do it. Mr. Henderson, Lester's former employer, owned the property free and clear. All Lester had to worry about each year were taxes and overhead.

"How many cameras will you need?" he asked.

"I'm not sure," I told him. "Probably two. Maybe three. You'll need to come over and take a look."

"Okay. Let me ask you a couple of questions, first. What are you going to use the tape for?"

"I don't know — does it matter?"

"Yeah. If you need broadcast quality tape, we ought to use a special camera. It's kinda big and bulky, so placement will be tough. Otherwise we can just rig up a couple of Camcorders."

"Gotcha. No, I just want the tape for my own use. Basically, I want a record of who's come around snooping while I'm away."

"Er, do you think someone will?" he asked, smelling adventure.

"Unfortunately, yes." I felt Lester deserved a little elaboration, so I continued. "He thinks I have something he wants. I don't, not anymore, but I need to know if he's come for it."

"Oh."

"Here's the tricky part, Lester. I'd like the camera to be activated by a motion detector. Is that possible?"

"Sure," he answered at once. "A lot of security systems are like that."

"Great. And I'd like the detector to be hooked up to some kind of alarm, inside my house — one that will wake me up when I go to bed. If he comes around in the middle of the night, I'd certainly appreciate the warning."

"Well ..." Lester said, thinking out loud, "I can do it, but I'll have to string about a mile of wire. It'll be kind of unsightly."

"I don't care. Just as long as it works."

"Oh, it'll work," he assured me. "Hey, this'll be neat! I'll bring some stuff with me tomorrow morning. I might even be able to get something hooked up by the time I leave."

"Good boy," I told him. "And you'll bill me?"

"Well, er —"

"Nothing doing," I said. "This isn't a favor. This is business. You bill me, okay? You're not a millionaire. Yet."

"Oh all right," he said wistfully. "But it sounds like a lot more fun than what I've been doing."

"There's nothing to say you can't have fun and get paid for it," I assured him. "Why, just look at what I do. I have a ball. But I still charge people."

"You don't exactly have a ball," he said prissily. "Last year you got shot. And you almost drowned. The year before —"

"Enough, already. I concede the point."

"You know," he sighed, "I'm really grateful that Mr. Henderson left me the business. Don't get me wrong. But it's awfully boring."

"Life is what you make it, kiddo," I told him, aware that I sounded more than a little like Dear Abby. "You'll figure out how to make it fun, if that's what you want."

"Yeah, I guess so," he said glumly. "See you tomorrow."

"Around seven?"

"Okay."

"Cheer up. Maybe you'll go into the security system business as a sideline. Think of my place as a trial run."

"Seven," he said heavily and hung up.

Ah, the burdens of wealth.

And suddenly there were no more calls to be placed, no more preparations to be made. There was just me and my empty house, the night dark and huge outside, and the year slipping away. I was so depressed I could have wept. The coincidence of my birthday, Christmas, and the dark dreariness of this time of year always does it to me. *In the bleak midwinter, frosty winds make moan.* Add to the above the freight of belief in a higher power that accompanies the season. I'd give a lot to believe, but I've seen too much cruelty and violence to fool myself into faith. Is there somewhere a method to all this madness? A pattern? A plan? In the last few years, I've come, sadly, to doubt it. And that's why Christmas is so hard on me. It's a ceremony of faith, a reaffirmation of belief that someone up there is taking care of us. Alas, I no longer believe that.

I poured another splash of Scotch and carried it in to my bedroom with me. Sensing distress, Repo waddled in with me and as I lay on the bed in the dark, he snuggled close. I sipped my Scotch and brooded, and before I knew it, there was the ghost of Jonna, knocking at memory's door again. Well, what had I expected? All right, I told myself with weary finality. Once more. I'd do this just once more — I would allow myself to feel all the guilt, the anger, and the shame associated with those last weeks with Jonna, and then I would not relive them again. I had successfully locked Jonna away for twenty-two years. I could do it again. Well, couldn't I?

It was late October of my college freshman year. I had won a scholarship to the University of Toronto to study English literature and philosophy. A little city unto itself, the campus was patterned after the British system, divided physically into colleges, each with its own cluster of buildings, and each with its own academic specialty. My college was Trinity, the oldest. I loved everything about the campus — the gargoyles that leered from unexpected places, the quiet, flower-filled quads, the cloisters, the newel post carved in the form of a dragon at the bottom of Victoria College's staircase, the magnificent stained-glass windows. And the libraries! There were twelve of them on campus, and I'd made a point to visit them all. I had a tiny apartment just off campus, in a neighborhood of old Victorian homes. I rode my bike everywhere and thought I was the luckiest person alive. I had even managed to forget Jonna through a combination of will power and total immersion in my studies. One night in October changed all that.

When the knock came on my door at quarter to nine, I was a little apprehensive. No one ever visited me here in my attic. I hadn't made any friends I cared to invite up to my tiny home, so I approached the door with caution.

"Who's there?" I called.

After a moment of silence, a voice answered, "Jonna."

Thinking someone was playing a joke on me, I wrenched open the door. And there she stood, dressed in jeans and an old red pullover sweater, suitcase in hand. For my part, I just stared.

"Oh, Caitlin," she said, and started to cry.

For a moment, I didn't know what to say. "Why are you here?" I managed finally. I had often fantasized about this moment — the moment when Jonna came back to me, never believing for a moment that it would become reality. But I've noticed that Fate has a nasty way of seeing that we get what we wish for. I was surprised that my reaction to Jonna was alarm and caution — in my fantasies, it has been passionate delight.

"I'm here because," she gulped, "well, I have nowhere else to go."

"I don't understand. Why don't you have anywhere else to go?"

"It's Kirk Ratliffe," she sobbed. "We went out together a few times and now he won't leave me alone."

My stomach clenched at this. "I know you went out with him," I said frostily. "And it was more than a few times. So what's the problem. Tell him to get lost. Isn't it a woman's prerogative to change her mind?"

"You don't understand," she said, her voice falling to a whisper. Her teeth began to chatter. "It . . . he isn't what I expected."

I found myself becoming exasperated, and as I usually do when annoyed, I fell back on sarcasm.

114

"Why not, Jonna? He has all the necessary equipment, doesn't he? What more did you expect? Roses? True love?"

This only made her sob harder. "Okay, I deserved that. But listen to me, Caitlin. Please. I never *let* him make love to me. He raped me. Every single time."

I felt sick. "What do you mean 'every single time.' Wasn't once enough?"

"He ... he apologized. Said he was drunk and got carried away. So I went out with him once more and he did it again. But he didn't have to!" Her eyes met mine. "The first time, last spring, I would have willingly gone to bed with him. I wanted to punish you. I wanted to find out what it was like so I could taunt you with it. I was angry with you. I was wrong. I'm sorry."

I forced my mind back to what she was telling me about Ratliffe. "So why didn't you go to the police?"

She laughed. "I tried. An officer came out to my aunt's place, but when I told him what had happened, and that Kirk Ratliffe was involved, he just put his notebook away. I guess he thought he was being kind to me when he told me to forget it. 'Don't make trouble for yourself,' he said."

"Okay," I said brutally. "So you didn't make trouble for yourself. Now what?"

"Now I can't get away from him. He follows me everywhere." She hugged herself. "I'm afraid he'll catch me alone where I can't ... I'm afraid ..." She trailed off.

"What do you want me to do?" I asked her, my heart beating double time. I wanted to hear it from her straight — I wanted her to ask me for help so I could refuse.

"Could you let me stay here a while? Just until I get a job and can save some money? Then I can get far, far away from him."

"Toronto's a big place," I told her. "A lot bigger than Ottawa. You don't need to run any farther if you don't want to. He'd never find you here," I said ambiguously, perfectly aware that I hadn't answered her question. I hated myself for doing it, but I wanted to hear her beg.

"Please," Jonna said. "Can I come in?"

The moonlight made her face all planes and angles and as I looked at her, I realized how much she had hurt me but how much I still wanted her. A part of me knew even then that if I let Jonna in, trouble was sure to follow. But I couldn't help myself. I had intended to send her away; instead, I did just the opposite. "All right," I said, and opened the door.

I don't remember what we talked about that evening, what we ate or drank, or how the time passed. What I do remember is that about midnight, Jonna crept from the couch into my bed.

"No, Jonna," I protested, dismayed.

"Why not?" she asked, her breath warm against my cheek. "You can't say that you don't want me."

"No, I can't say that," I admitted. My damp palms and accelerated heartbeat attested to my desire for her.

"Well, then?"

What was I to say? The enormity of my protest, the reason why I didn't want her in my bed was so complex and convoluted that I knew I could never sum it up in a few words. Still, I tried. "You're . . . you're not here because you ran to me," I began. "You're here because you ran away from him."

"Don't be silly," she said, deliberately misunderstanding. "Of course I'm here because of you." She laughed then, and traced the outline of my lips with one finger. And because I wanted her so much, I gave up. *I want this,* I told myself. *I deserve it. I don't care that she doesn't love me, that she's using me because she's broke. Hell, I'm using her too. I want this, dammit, and if she's offering, I'm taking. All I have to remember is that she doesn't care about me, and I don't care about her. If I remember that, I won't get hurt again.* And with that, I abandoned all resistance. I was seventeen years old, and except for some pretty straightforward masturbation, I hadn't had the opportunity to get acquainted with what my body wanted. I desperately envied my straight classmates the opportunities they had to date, to be intimate with each other, to learn all about sex. Hell, they had not only unlimited opportunities, but society's sanction! I had no such advantages. Except for Jonna, any of the attractions I had felt for other girls had been kept strictly to myself. This wasn't exactly what I had envisioned for my first lesbian sexual experience, but I decided I'd take it anyhow.

Turning on my side, I put my hand on her arm. She had unbraided her hair and it lay in a silken wing over her shoulder. I slipped my hand under her hair until I held the warm nape of her neck against my palm. With a start, I realized that I had fantasized precisely this scene. I began to tremble, and when she bent to kiss me, it was too much. I closed my mind down and abandoned myself to the rush of feeling that surged like a riptide through my body. *To hell with the consequences,* I thought. *To hell with everything.*

Later that night, while Jonna slept, I lay awake feeling soiled and ashamed. The physical experience had been better, more powerful than anything I had fantasized, but unfortunately, it had been only half of what I longed for. Romantic fool that I was, I still believed there ought to be something other than hormones that brought people together. I think that if Jonna had wanted me even a little, I could have salvaged some self-respect. But either she was a terrible actress or she didn't think it necessary to feign desire. I might have been naive and inexperienced, but I knew after the first kiss that she wasn't in my bed because she had the hots for me. Nope. I knew she was only paying the rent, and that saddened and disgusted me. But what was I to do? Just thinking about what we had done made my body respond all over again and I knew that if she were to awaken that very moment and touch me, my reservations and resistance would melt away. I knew that as long as Jonna was here, I would return to this bed, to her, again and again and that made me feel alarmed and ashamed. *Go away,* I said to her silently. *Go soon.*

I needn't have worried. Fate, as I've said, has a way of making your wishes come true.

Six weeks later, I started off for class during the tail-end of a blizzard that had raged half the night. Walking the ten blocks to the edge of campus took me an hour and when I ran into the shelter of the new athletic building, winded and half frozen, I realized that there were no cars on the street. Then, as I peered outside, the snow simply ... stopped, and the sun shone from an impossibly blue sky. I pushed open the door and walked back out onto the sidewalk, looking around. Last night's wind had whipped the snowbanks into three-foot mounds, the tops of parked cars barely peeking above them. With a laugh, I set off for home. There would be no classes today. On the way, I stopped at the bakery on the corner and bought a cheese and a prune danish. Jonna wouldn't be able to go job hunting, I realized, and with guilty delight I looked forward to surprising her in bed.

I certainly did.

Throwing open the door to my apartment, I kicked off my boots, dropped my backpack, and without taking off my parka, bounded toward the bed. And stopped short. For there, tangled in the sheets, were Jonna and Kirk Ratliffe. When they heard me come in they sat up, clearly surprised. Jonna clutched the sheet to her chest in a parody of modesty, while Kirk, recognizing me, leered and didn't even bother to cover himself. I was so stunned that for a moment I thought that perhaps I was on the wrong street. Maybe I'd wandered into the wrong apartment. Then I thought frantically that this must be a dream, for surely this was as bad as any nightmare. And then I was all out of modes of denial. *Yes, this is really happening*, I told myself. *You interrupted Jonna and Kirk fucking in your bed. And it sure doesn't look like rape, does it? No sirree. How very interesting.*

"You have five minutes to get your clothes on," I

told both of them. "I'm going downstairs to the neighbor's. If you're not out of here by then, I'm calling the cops."

Kirk laughed. "What will you tell them?"

I turned on him, unable to keep the rage and shame I felt out of my voice. "Don't fuck with me, Ratliffe. It won't work." I picked up his jeans and threw them at him. "Five minutes." Then I turned my rage on Jonna. "You miserable whore! You'll put out for whoever has something you want. Is that how you think you'll pay your way through life? With your cunt?"

Ratliffe was wisely silent. Jonna, however, looked up at me, eyes pleading. "This isn't what you think," she said in a rush. "Please, let me explain."

But I was in no mood for explanations. Picking up a handful of her clothes, I fired them at her. "No more! Just get dressed and go. And take your crap with you because what you leave behind I'm throwing out in the snow."

They were gone in four minutes. From my downstairs neighbor's front window I watched them go, and when they were gone, I went slowly back to my attic, my legs so heavy I could hardly walk. For about an hour I sat in the one easy chair I possessed, still dressed in my parka, too numb to feel anything. I decided I wanted to stay that way so I hunted down the single bottle of liquor I had in my apartment — a half-full bottle of vodka — poured eight ounces in a tall water glass, filled it with orange juice, and started to drink.

The phone rang and I reached to take it off the hook, dropping the receiver on the floor. Lifting the glass to my lips, I took a huge swallow — the vodka couldn't do its work fast enough as far as I was concerned. How long did it take to get drunk, anyhow? I had no idea. So I sat and drank, grimacing. Finally, after what seemed like years, lips and fingers numb, I staggered to the couch, head spinning. Pulling the afghan over my feet, I burrowed into my parka, feeling as though I were sliding down a long, slippery slope to a very dark destination. Grief, sharp and bright as a blade, pierced my heart, but I let my rage turn it aside. *No. I will not cry*, I told myself stubbornly. *I will not cry. Not for her. Not ever.* And I never did.

Now, twenty-two years later I lay in another bed, older but no wiser. I still had no answers for Jonna's behavior. What had she been about to tell me when I threw her out? I never knew. I refused to talk to her on the phone and burned her letters unread. Eventually she gave up and went away. Later — eleven years later — when she had telephoned me, taking me by surprise, I had been rude, sarcastic, and unfeeling. I hadn't allowed her to even say why she had called. I wasn't proud of that. And now she very likely was dead and whatever I needed to hear from her, whatever she had tried to tell me, was dead with her.

I finished the last of my Scotch and turned out the light. Oblivion — the same dark place that had beckoned me the day I had found Jonna and Kirk together — crooked its finger again, but I resisted getting up to pour more Scotch. Instead, I lay in the dark and waited for sleep. It was a long time coming.

MONDAY

Chapter 7

Next morning, feeling as though I'd been exhumed, I staggered out of bed, threw on a down vest, laced on my Brooks, and coaxed my MG into sputtering life. Yawning, I drove to the corner bakery for some apple fritters, tossed them into the back seat, and navigated a bleary-eyed return to *chez moi*. As I turned onto my street off Oak Bay Avenue, I noticed my neighbor across the street and two doors down had a visitor from Ontario and that the visitor was engaged in car repairs. My antennae stirred for a moment before I remembered that both sons lived in the east. Presumably this was one of the prodigals, returned for the festive season. Such enterprise. I think I'd have called the automobile club. Who wants to lie on the cold pavement at seven-thirty in the morning? I was just thinking about the folly of this, when I noticed Lester's jeep turning into my driveway.

"Breakfast," I told him, holding up the paper sack I'd brought from the bakery.

"Er, thanks," he said, eyeing the bag suspiciously as he climbed out of the jeep. Dressed in clean, pressed jeans and a dark green wool shirt, he looked as dapper as ever. "But I've already eaten. Scrambled eggs and toast. And tea."

"Shoot, Lester, you're no fun," I teased, reminding him of a past breakfast he'd watched me devour. "I thought we'd share some batter-fried rock cod. And cole slaw." I joined him in the driveway.

He looked ill. "Your stomach may be able to stand that stuff in the morning, but I have to eat my meals in order. Batter-fried rock cod is definitely lunch," he asserted.

I threw an arm around his shoulders. "Tut, tut. So young but so set in your ways. C'mon in, Lester. Bring your stuff. I'll put the kettle on so you can make yourself a second cup of tea. I'm going to start coffee and have a shower."

Half an hour later, I pulled on a comfy lavender wool crewneck sweater over a white turtleneck, zipped up my faded old jeans, found some nice woolly socks, and padded out to the kitchen. I needed to see the report that South Van had produced. If I was going to find Kirk before he found Jory, I needed something to work with. Maybe he'd left something behind, or dropped something. But why should South Van tell me anything, anyhow? With no great hope, I dialed the number Sandy had given me, identified myself, asked for Officer Lynne Hadley and settled in to wait. To my surprise, she answered at once.

"Hi. I've been expecting your call."

"You have?"

"Yeah. Sandy Alexander's a friend of mine. He mentioned that this case was special to you." She lowered her voice. "He trained me. So I feel I owe him."

"Oh." Sandy never told me that.

"I made a copy of the report," she continued, *sotto voce*. "I have the photos too. I can courier them to you if you get them right back to me. They won't be missed for a day or two."

"Can you fax me the report?" I asked. "You could courier the photos. But I'd really like to see the report ... well, now."

"Yeah, I can do that. I'm going out on patrol in about an hour. I can do it then."

"Thanks. I really appreciate this." I gave her the local copy shop's fax number. "Listen, would you mind if I called you and talked to you about what you saw at the scene?"

"I don't mind a bit," she said cheerily. "Call me at this number — it's my home. I'll be there after eleven."

I scribbled the number on a pad beside the phone. "Thanks, Lynne."

"No problem," she said. "Sandy told me a lot about you. I'd like to meet you if you ever get over here."

I was stunned. Was this lady making a pass at me? "Well, I might just do that. I'd like to see the clothes and things that were left in the motel room."

"I'd be happy to help," she said. "Just let me know when you're coming."

"Hey, I will. Thanks again."

What on earth *had* Sandy told her about me? Under other circumstances, I might have been interested. But I was not in the mood for flirtation. I had enough on my mind. And there *was* Tonia, I reminded myself sternly.

I poured myself another cup of coffee and doodled on my yellow tablet. Oh, what the hell. Dialing the number for Ottawa directory assistance, I asked for Viola Ratliffe's phone number. Emboldened by the ease with which I got it, I then asked for the Andresson's number, thinking they probably had a separate line. They did. I copied down both numbers then sat looking uncertainly at them. What if none of them would talk to me? I desperately needed someone to confirm or deny Jory's veracity.

But who to try first — Grandma or Mrs. Andresson? My gut told me the housekeeper, so with no great optimism, I dialed the Andresson's number. I had no idea what her relationship had been with Jory (I was sure she hadn't enjoyed being addressed as Nimue for a month, or searching for Jory's UFO) so I decided a little prevarication was in order.

"Mrs. Andresson?" I asked in my best public servant voice.

"Yes?" a cautious voice replied.

"This is Caitlin Rogers at Child Protective Services in Victoria."

"Oh no. Has something happened to Jory?"

Aha! Was that concern I detected? Score one for my side. "No, not exactly. Something has happened to her mother, though. That's why we have the child."

"Why, what's happened to Jonna?" she asked, her voice flat. Better and better. She liked the kid but didn't care for the mom.

"She apparently was in an altercation with her husband in a motel room on the mainland. Both adults seem to have disappeared and abandoned the child."

"Oh my Lord," she said, distress evident in her voice. "This will kill Mrs. Ratliffe. She's not well, you know — her heart — and she just dotes on that little girl. What's going to become of her?"

"We wonder that too, Mrs. Andresson. Is Mrs. Ratliffe the child's only living relative?"

"Yes. And she's in no condition to care for a child — don't go thinking that. Nor are we, Everett and I, that is. We're almost as broken-down as she is."

"Well, not to worry right now, Mrs. Andresson," I soothed. "The little girl is fine. We may petition to place her in a foster home, but first we need to know a little more about her."

"Poor little thing. She's been through so much! And now this — abandoned!"

"Yes, it certainly is a shame," I agreed. "She seems very bright."

"Bright? The child is a genius. Before she had her heart trouble, Mrs. Ratliffe had her tested one time. The had her at the university for the whole day giving her those whatchamacallit tests."

"IQ tests? Intelligence tests?"

"Yes, that's right. And it's such a shame that her mother never even sent her to school."

For a moment, I was speechless. "But she can read," I said lamely.

"Of course she can read. Write, too. Her grandma and I taught her. And Mr. Andresson taught her her sums and to play the piano. When we had her, that is. We figured that if she could read and write and do sums, well, she could learn to do harder things on her own. Because that no-good mother of hers wasn't going to help."

"You really are to be commended," I said sincerely. "But why was the mother so ... difficult?"

"Hmmf," she said. "I guess you'll find out anyhow so there's no harm in telling you. The mother was a drinker. She had a hard enough time taking care of herself."

"Why on earth didn't she just leave the child with you?" I wondered aloud.

Mrs. Andresson sighed. "Oh, she'd sober up when Kirk — that's her husband — was due to get out of jail. Then she'd come to get Jory and they'd take off to be one big happy family. But that never lasted. She'd always backslide."

"Start drinking again?"

"Yes. Then they'd fight, and well, that's probably enough said. It was awfully hard on Jory."

I decided to go for broke. "Mrs. Andresson, Jory shows evidence of having been beaten. And frankly, we're wondering ..."

"About other things?" she asked. "Thank the Lord someone is finally wondering. I tried and tried to tell Mrs. Ratliffe that her son wasn't being a fit father to Jory, but she wanted it to be all Jonna's fault. And it wasn't, you know. Both of them took their bad moods out on Jory —"

"You mean they both beat her?"

"Well, she said her mother used to slap her when she was drinking — she didn't want Jory bothering her — but it was Kirk, her father, who beat her."

I felt sick. "Tell me about the 'other things.'"

"They've been going on for about three years, as nearly as I can figure it. Kirk started out just ... touching Jory when she was sleeping, the girl said. Then he started coming into her bed when Jonna was passed out and making her ... do things to him."

I felt sick. "How far did it go? Did he rape her?"

"No. And I'm sure she would have told me. But they've been gone for about a month, so ..."

"Yes, well, we'll see that she gets a proper medical examination," I said, lapsing into my Child Protective Services persona again. "Did Jory tell her mother about these things?"

"She said she tried, but her mother wouldn't listen. And of course, there was no point in trying to tell her grandma," she added bitterly.

"Oh?"

"Mrs. Ratliffe loved the little girl dearly, but she would never have believed that her son would do anything so awful."

"But wasn't he in and out of jail a lot?"

"Yes, but mainly for fighting when he was drunk and stealing cars. That sort of thing."

Good old boy mischief — the things he'd been doing since he was an adolescent. "I'm very glad she had someone to tell."

Mrs. Andresson sighed. "For all the good it did."

"Yes, it did," I reassured her. "Now that we know the situation, we're going to recommend that she be neither reunited with her parents, if they are located, nor returned to her grandmother." This of course was utter nonsense, but I was counting on the fact that Mrs. Andresson didn't know the difference. "Our primary concern is to keep her safe."

"Thank you," Mrs. Andresson sniffled a little. "She deserves better than she's had."

I had to ask this question. "There's just one thing that concerns me. Sometimes Jory seems to, well, tell some pretty fanciful stories. Why, she said she saw a UFO last night."

Mrs. Andresson laughed. "She's testing you."

"Testing me?"

"Yes. That's how she worked her way into telling me about her father molesting her. She flat out made up a make-believe world with some prince who was on a quest to find a magic sword. A magic sword which would keep him safe from an evil magician who turned out to be the prince's father. Yes, I remember that story very well. I just told Mr. Andresson to be patient with her. And she played the UFO trick on us, too."

"I see," I said slowly. "Did her father know about these games?"

"Oh yes. They drove him about crazy. The last couple of years when she had to live with them, she just refused to be herself, Jory. Wouldn't even answer to her name. The beatings began about then. I guess Kirk just couldn't cope with her."

"Well, it seems that he found another way to cope, to have power over her," I remarked bitterly.

"That's it, isn't it?" Mrs. Andresson remarked. "He was always like that, always a bully. Always wanted to make people do what *he* wanted."

Poor thwarted bully — neither his wife nor his child would obey him. Well, he'd found a way to deal with each of them — kill the wife and molest the daughter. Except Jory had gotten away.

"Thank you, Mrs. Andresson," I concluded. "I'm very glad I called you instead of Mrs. Ratliffe."

"I'm sure that would have been the proper thing to do, her being the little girl's relative and all, but —"

"But we learned what we needed to from you," I hurriedly assured her.

"Oh yes. You wouldn't have gotten far with Mrs. Ratliffe. Did Jory —"

"She urged us to call you, and not her grandma," I invented.

"I knew she was smart," she said, then fell silent. "Do you think, well, if she's placed with a foster family —"

"Of course you can talk to her," I anticipated. "Just as soon as she's settled. And thank you again."

"Well, all right then," she said and hung up.

I sat back, doodling on my yellow pad, feeling about an inch high. Even *I* had begun to doubt Jory. Jeez, the kid sure needed some friends.

"So how's it going?" I asked Lester as I plucked my jacket from the coat tree.

"Fine," he said. "I'll just finish stringing the wiring inside, then position the camera out under the eaves. I've got another one to install at the back door, then we're in business. You can pop the cassettes out and look at them when you come home at night."

"Tell me how they work."

"Well, I've rigged them so they operate on the same principle as the motion detectors on burglar alarms. Whenever anyone enters the path of the beam, the camera starts rolling. I've adjusted the beam so wandering cats won't set the camera off. That's all there is to it," he said modestly.

"You're a genius!" I told him, just to see him blush. "Got to go out for a bit. See you in an hour or so."

He pulled his Walkman out of his pocket, clapped the earphones on his head, and went to work.

I drove to the PDQ Copy Shoppe under a sky the color of an eggplant. More rain and gloom — why not? And sure enough, as I maneuvered the MG into the parking lot behind the Bank of Nova Scotia, the heavens rumbled and a nasty cold drizzle began. Muttering, I zipped my bomber jacket a little higher and sprinted across the street. By the time I had retrieved the fax from Lynne Hadley and had made my way back to my car, the drizzle was a full-fledged rain. I felt my spirits sag and told myself firmly not to be such an ass. This longing for light and warmth was probably just a phase I was going through — the psychic equivalent of thumb-sucking. It would probably pass, as did most other things. But in the meantime, it was a terribly lonely affliction — after all, who could I possibly tell?

Trying to cheer myself up, I hummed a verse from Ezra Pound's satire of that old English paean to spring, "Summer is Icumen In," which irreverent old Ezra had entitled "Ancient Music."

"Winter is icumen in
Lhude sing Goddamn,
Passeth bus and sloppeth us,
An ague hath my ham!
Sing: Goddamn."

But it didn't work. Instead, my masochistic mind
dredged up another refrain, one that it found
infinitely more pleasing:

"Blow, blow thou western wind,
That the small rain down can rain;
Christ, that my love were in my arms
And I in my bed again."

Very good, Reece. I snorted. There's nothing like
a liberal dollop of self-pity. Truly character-building.
So now you have Jonna tied round your neck like an
albatross. Well, you did it to yourself, you know. You
could have let her talk. You could have gotten in
touch with her yourself. Hell, did you think she'd
live forever? Or you? What were you saving the
occasion for — your dotage? She's very likely dead
and now you'll never know what she wanted to tell
you. The truth, presumably. And that's something
you'll just have to live with, kiddo.

But the sight I saw as I approached my house
drove all this self-indulgent blather clear out of my
head. A white van sat in the driveway. The front
passenger door was open, as though someone had
been in too great a hurry to close it. A terrible
premonition seized me and I began to shiver. Then I
saw — face down in the mud the body of a small
woman in jeans and a tan down vest, a slender

woman, a woman I knew well. I know I yelled
something but I can't remember what it was. Maybe
it was just her name. Gray. Nor can I remember
how I parked my car or crossed the yard to her
side. Hell, maybe I just levitated. Shaking, I knelt in
the mud and turned her enough to feel for the pulse
in her neck. As I did, I saw the puddle of rain and
blood in which her head lay, and the pale, pale cast
to her skin, and I did something I haven't done
since I was a child. I prayed. *Please, please let her
be alive. This ought to be me lying here. So I'll make
a deal with you. Let her live and next time I get into
a scrape, you can have me. No arguments, no
pleading. You can just flat out have me. But not her.
Not Gray.* Gently, I put my fingers under her collar,
against the warm skin of her neck, feeling for a
pulse.

"Lester!" I yelled. "Get out here!" But there was
no response. Dammit, where was he? His jeep was
still here. And then I remembered — the damned
Walkman. He was inside happily humming away
stringing wire while Gray was dying. "LESTER!" I
screamed.

I closed my eyes and prayed again and suddenly,
there it was. But faint, so faint. God, had I
imagined it? No. Under my fingers I felt the
fluttering of Gray's life. And then Lester was on the
front porch, earphones around his neck, a puzzled
expression on his face.

"Call 911!" I yelled.

Without a word, he turned and ran into the
house.

* * * * *

Sandy met me in one of the doctor's offices at Jubilee Hospital. I leaned against the wall, hands in my pockets, fighting the rage building up inside me.

"It was Ratliffe," I said.

He raised an eyebrow but wisely said nothing.

"It *was*," I insisted. "Jory's backpack was on the floor of the van. Gray must have brought her to my place for some reason. My guess is that he had my house staked out, recognized Jory, and grabbed her. Crap, Sandy, of course it was Ratliffe — who else could it have been? Have you got an APB out for his arrest?"

Sandy shrugged. "It's one explanation," he agreed. "Certainly someone assaulted your friend. And that someone probably took the child. But Caitlin, no one saw what happened."

"Gray saw."

"Yes. But Gray's unconscious," he reminded me gently. "And until she wakes up and tells us, we can't do anything."

"Shit!" I yelled, and kicked an office chair, sending it across the room. "Be officious, then. I'll handle things myself. What you *can* do for me, though, is to arrange that I can see Gray whenever I want. Do you think you can manage that?" I asked him unkindly. I walked away without waiting for his answer.

As I approached Gray's room, Lester raised his eyes from a perusal of his Topsiders. Shifting uneasily in his chair, he gave me a miserable, guilty look. I knew that he blamed himself for what had happened to Gray but I didn't have the emotional reserves to take care of him right now. I was terrified at the prospect that she might die.

"The doctor was just here," he said quietly. "There's been no change. She's still unconscious."

I squeezed his shoulder and he hung his head again, hands clasped between his knees, eyes on his shoes. "Wait for me, will you?" I asked him.

"Sure," he said in a barely audible voice.

I pulled open the heavy door and slipped inside.

Gray's presence in that bed hit me like a physical blow. It was so ... wrong seeing her lying there pale and still, eyes closed. The body really is just a vessel for the spirit, I realized with startling poignancy, and it wrung my heart to see Gray like this. She was so slight that her body made hardly a bulge in the blankets, but that body was not Gray. A machine beeped at her bedside, chronicling her heartbeats, but that, too, had nothing to do with Gray. It was her soul, her essence, that was absent. With a great sense of helplessness, I took a chair and sat beside her. I wanted desperately to talk to her and considered holding one of her hands in mine, but this was a liberty I felt I could not take with her.

"Gray," I whispered. "Where are you?" I felt acutely powerless. Everything I had ever read about coma victims flashed through my mind, and I decided then and there that I would talk to Gray just as though she were conscious. Hell, for all I knew she could hear every word. So I started. I told her all about Jonna — how she had come into my life, what had happened between us. I had just started to tell her about Ratliffe and Jonna when the door opened.

"I'm going to get some supper," Lester said. "Want me to get some for you?"

I looked at my watch in amazement. Where had the hours gone? I realized in a rush of panic that I had been inaccessible all day — what if Francis had called? Hell, if Jory just disappeared off the face of the earth, all this would be for nothing. More now than ever, I needed to find Ratliffe. Because finding him was finding Jory.

"I'll get supper for us," I told him. "C'mon in."

Sheepishly, he obeyed.

"Sit here," I told him. "And talk to her."

"Er, about what?'" he asked, adjusting his glasses nervously.

"About anything. Just talk."

"All right," he agreed. "But what if, you know, the nurses ask me to leave. I'm not family."

"Neither am I," I said grimly. "But I asked Sergeant Alexander to arrange it that I could visit her. Just lie and tell them you're my brother."

He adjusted his glasses again in fussy disapproval but didn't object. I left him telling Gray about the photography business.

A thick fog had crept in from the sea, and as I drove down Estevan to a fish and chips place I knew that served good food, I felt swallowed up in the gray maw of some beast. Driving was so disorienting that I began to be afraid that I would rear-end one of the cars that were parked at the curb. Crossing intersections was out of the question. So I gave up and pulled my car off the street into what seemed to be a school parking lot. A single sickly orange sodium vapor light burned on a tall pole and I thought I knew where I was — the Estevan Street Public School. If so, the fish and chips place was just around the corner. I got out of my MG, zipped my jacket against the fog, and set off into the swirling mist. Bad move.

I hadn't gone more than a hundred paces before I realized I must have turned the wrong way out of the school parking lot. The fish and chips place was nowhere in sight. Nor indeed were any of the businesses that shared the block with it. I swore under my breath and cursed the useless streetlights that shone overhead like pale opal moons. I walked on another hundred paces and was only mildly alarmed when the pavement changed to grass. *The park at the end of the block,* I told myself. *Damn. Better turn around and go back.* Then I paused. Wasn't that a snatch of conversation I'd just heard off to my right? Hmmm. Could it be that I was on the wrong block? Was Estevan just around the corner? Dithering, I peered into the fog and decided to walk a hundred paces to my right. That should bring me either to Estevan Street, or to the public parking lot at the beach.

Counting my steps carefully, I set off through the fog. Ninety-eight, ninety-nine, one hundred. Nope. No Estevan Street. Worse yet, no beach parking lot. Shit. The footing was still grass — where the hell was I? Beach Park wasn't this big. Okay, I decided, time to turn around and go back. Lester would be wondering what had become of me.

I turned, thinking to simply retrace my steps, and froze in amazement. A wind from the sea thinned the billows of fog a little, and I saw that I was certainly not in Beach Park. Where I was instead, I saw with a prickling of fear, was a graveyard. I looked down and, heart thudding, realized that I was standing directly on someone's grave. Kneeling, I peered through the mist for the grave marker and found it just in front of my sneakers where I would have cracked my shins on it had I continued walking. Scrambling off the grave into the grass, I stood up cautiously, wiping my hands on my jeans. Okay, now what? As far as I knew, there was no graveyard anywhere near Estevan Street.

The wind gusted again, shredding the fog a little more, and I gasped. I was in the middle of a thicket of graves — tiny plaques set flush with the earth, small headstones that barely reached my knees, enormous markers that towered over my head. How on earth had I gotten here without tripping over a headstone and braining myself, I wondered. Off to my left, a somber granite angel, wings furled, presided over a quintet of graves, and I walked toward her down a grassy aisle. But before I got there, I saw motion out of the corner of my eye and turned. A woman in jeans and a leather jacket stood between two graves. On one side of her was a taller, slender woman with straight raven hair. On the other side was a girl of about ten, hair braided. This was a pretty strange time to be visiting the family grave, I thought. Still, they could be lost in the fog, like me. I was about to call out to them, to ask for directions, when to my amazement, the woman in the leather jacket held out her hands, the other two took them, and they vanished. Just like that. Gone. Disappeared. I blinked in disbelief, expecting the fog to part and reveal them again, but it didn't. What *did* happen was a very curious thing.

The fog settled down on me like a feather comforter and I distinctly heard two things: the mournful sound of a warning buoy, and the *whooshing* sound the sea makes as it breaks on a pebble beach. I thought again of the lines from "Dover Beach":

"Listen! You hear the grating roar
Of pebbles which the waves draw back, and fling,
At their return, up the high strand,
Begin and cease, and then again begin,
With tremulous cadence slow, and bring
The eternal note of sadness in."

The buoy hooted once more and this time, when the wind changed, I smelled cedars, damp earth, and the unmistakable tang of the sea. I stood perfectly still, hair lifting on the back of my neck because wherever I was, I was not on safe, comfortable Estevan Street in Oak Bay. In fact, I doubted I was in Oak Bay at all.

Throat too dry to speak, I swallowed noisily. For some reason I could not name, I peeled back my sleeve and pressed the button that illuminated the time on my digital watch. To my consternation, I saw that it had stopped. The numbers read 7:22:51.

I had left the hospital just after seven. Given that it had taken me fifteen or twenty minutes to drive to the school parking lot, my watch must have stopped soon after I wandered into the graveyard. I patted the bulge my .357 made in the small of my back, but for some reason, it's presence didn't make me feel a bit better.

The wind fanned my hair and the fog parted again. Hearing a scuffling noise behind me, I turned. The trio I had seen by the granite angel was there again, holding hands, backs to me, walking away. I heaved a huge sigh of relief — they hadn't vanished at all. It had simply been a trick of the mist.

"Hey!" I croaked. But they gave no indication they had heard. "Wait, I'm lost! How do you get out of here?"

With a soughing *whoosh*, the wind blew the last streamers of fog away, and I saw with horror that I was standing on the edge of a precipice. Below me was the sea. About half a mile out, there was an amber light atop a bell buoy, and by the light of the full moon I could make out the faint phosphorescence of the surf as it ebbed down a pebble beach. About fifty feet below me was a tiny horseshoe-shaped bay. Where in hell *was* I, anyhow?

Then, out of the corner of my eye, I saw the trio from the graveyard come strolling toward the cliff. I almost called out to them to be careful for God's sake, when I realized that I could see *through* the woman in the leather jacket. My tongue stuck to the roof of my mouth as, holding her companions' hands, she glided over the edge of the cliff. And as they passed between me and a fat moon that lay like a bright silver dollar just above the horizon, I realized that all three of them were as insubstantial as mist. Like figures in a dream, they walked onto the moon's laddered trail and were swallowed up in brightness. My teeth started to chatter. "No," I said aloud in denial.

And then I ran. From the cliff edge and the thing I had seen that wasn't possible, from the graveyard that shouldn't be there, and from the face of the woman in the leather jacket. Because just before she stepped off the edge of the cliff, she half turned to me and I caught a glimpse of her face. It was a face I knew very well, a face I saw in the mirror every morning. It was my face.

I ran until my lungs screamed at me to stop, until I whooped and moaned for breath, until my legs felt mired in mud. Then, I fell to my hands and knees, gagging, nose running, crying unashamedly. After a few minutes when my breathing had slowed and I'd wiped my nose on my sleeve, I looked down and realized I was kneeling on the gravel of a parking lot. I picked two particularly sharp pieces of rock out of my palm and, long past amazement, stood up. Overhead a single sickly orange sodium vapor light burned. In front of me was my car.

"No," I said again. Closing my eyes, I wondered for a fleeting second if I had suffered a fugue, a lapse in consciousness. No, I decided, I hadn't. What then? It had all seemed so *real*. Gray, I thought. Gray will know the truth of this. And with that thought, a conviction, bright as a spear of lightning sizzled through my brain: *Gray was all right*. Somehow I knew this. Just as I knew that she could explain what had happened to me in the fog. I knew this with the part of me that knew beyond a doubt that Gray really was a witch and could talk to animals. I guess she would have called it my spirit.

Fishing the car keys out of my pocket, I unlocked the door and coaxed the MG to shuddering life. As I did so, I looked at my watch — 7:23:13. It was working again, and what it told me was that twenty-four seconds had passed. With a sense of wonder, I thought again of the stone angel, the cedar snags, the bell buoy, the woman who looked like me. What did it all mean?

With great care, I drove out of the school lot and onto Estevan Street, retracing my route until I came to the traffic lights at Oak Bay Avenue. The fog wasn't nearly as dense here, away from the ocean, and I was easily able to find my way to McDonald's. I ordered supper for Lester and me, put it on the seat beside me, and maneuvered myself back into traffic, heading for Jubilee Hospital.

Lester met me as I came around the corner and down the hall to Gray's room.

"It's amazing!" he declared. "She just opened her eyes, said 'Caitlin,' and sat up. I called the doctor and we nearly had to hold her down. She's okay!"

I didn't have the heart to tell him that I wasn't surprised. "Great!" I enthused, handing him the McDonald's bag. "Save something for me," I told him. "I'll go see her now." He took the bag and trotted down to the waiting area, humming happily to himself.

When I opened the door, Gray was dressed, sitting on the side of the bed. She looked at me out of eyes as black as anthracite. *I love her,* I thought fiercely, wondering how I had never realized this before, and how inadequate the verb *love* was anyhow. Because I loved Gray in a way that I had never loved anyone before. Why is it that it takes almost losing someone to sharpen the focus of our affections? All I knew was that if she had died, I would have lost one of my anchors, my north star. I had never met anyone about whom I could say that. Not until I had known Gray. How could I not have realized before how dear she had become to me, how necessary? Yet this was so different from what I felt for Tonia that I hesitated to call it love at all. What the hell was it? Crossing the room, I sat on the bed beside her, looking into her eyes. The distance Gray always liked to keep around her, her separateness, prevented me from doing what I would have done with anyone else — taking her hands in mine, touching her for reassurance that she was indeed alive.

"Where were you?" I asked her finally.

"A familiar place," she said, her voice quiet. "A place I know well. I have been there several times before. This time, I thought I might stay." She gestured around her. "All this was very far away."

"Why didn't you stay?" I asked, mouth dry.

She looked at me intently. "Someone made a bargain for me. I returned to fulfill it."

I shivered, wanting to ask her what I had longed to ask for years: *Who are you?* Instead, I asked another question. "Did you want to stay?"

She did not answer me. "Tell me what you want to know," she said, smiling a little.

I told her about getting lost in the fog, about what I saw, about having been gone only twenty-four seconds according to my watch.

"What do you think it means?" she asked me.

I shivered again. "I don't know. I don't want to think about it."

"You will not learn the answer by thinking about it," she said. "Tonight, tomorrow, the day after, your spirit will speak to you when you are thinking about something else. When your mind is engaged in thought, freeing the spirit pathway, the answer will come to you." She looked at me reproachfully, raising a finger to tap my breastbone. "Do you not know by now that you have all the answers in here?" Then she tapped my head, just over one eyebrow. "Not here."

"I guess not."

She climbed down from the bed and walked to the closet. "I have signed myself out, satisfying the hospital's desire for self-protection," she informed me, slipping into her down vest. "Shall we go?"

"Go? Go where?" I asked stupidly.

"Why, in search of the child," she said to me. "Where else?"

Jory. Of course. "I'd ... forgotten about her," I admitted sheepishly.

"Meeting the dead makes one forgetful of the living." She walked to the door. "Still, while we are here among them, we must attend to promises we have made. Come. Let us prepare to discharge our obligations."

What as she hinting at? And what had she meant by meeting the dead? Was that who I had seen in the fog? And what bargain had forced her to return? I wanted to ask her to wait, to talk to me, to explain, but I knew she wouldn't. Over the years, she turned aside all my requests for elucidation of the non-rational with smiles and enigmatic sayings. I certainly wasn't about to disgrace myself by asking again. Gray always made me feel like a dolt, a clod, a thick-skulled fool. Well, I'd just have to figure things out for myself.

Chapter 8

I sent Lester home with Gray to make sure she really *was* all right. He had specific instructions to heft forkfuls of hay for the bay pony and do any of the other fetching and carrying Gray required. Amazingly, she agreed. I'd been clobbered on the head myself and recalled vividly the percussion section that had played inside my skull for days.

I fed my own menagerie, and while a pot of coffee was brewing, I scrambled a few eggs. With a lined yellow tablet in front of me, I sat at the kitchen table nibbling toast and making a list of the things I needed to do. I was well into it when the phone rang so I plucked the receiver off the wall with more than a little irritation. If I was ever to catch up with Ratliffe, I couldn't waste time chatting on the phone.

"Sweetie," a tenor voice cooed. "You're soooo hard to find!"

"Talk to me, Francis," I said, heartbeat accelerating.

"What a naughty fellow your Kirk Ratliffe has been — ever so many arrests and convictions."

"Tell me something I don't know, Francis. Something that will help me find him. Pronto."

"So testy, so importunate," he chided. "Very well. Is your pencil poised?"

"It is."

"He left a paper trail across Canada. Mostly gasoline purchases. Although he did spend over three hundred dollars at an outdoor outfitter on the mainland. Oh, you may be interested to know that this particular credit card is actually a debit card for a small brokerage account. Apparently his mother puts a certain amount into the account monthly. Isn't that nice?"

"Continue," I said between clenched teeth.

"You're fearsome when you're like this," he said. "I'm positively quaking. But I shall continue. His most recent purchases were in Chemainus. He bought two meals. Today."

"Two meals? You're sure it wasn't three?"

"I am most definitely sure," he said, miffed.

Two meals. For himself and Jory, I guessed. But what the hell was Ratliffe doing in Chemainus? That was, oh, fifty miles up island.

"Anything else?"

"And he bought two ferry tickets. Destination — Thetis Island." Two ferry tickets. What further proof did I need?

"Thetis? There's nothing there. What the hell could he be up to, anyhow?"

"Well," Francis said loftily, "there may be nothing for him on Thetis, but there might well be on Ciel Island."

"Ciel Island?" And then it hit me, what Jory had told me: "He said we'd go and live in Heaven." And *ciel* was the French word for heaven! Yes. He'd take her there.

"Yes. The Ratliffes own it. It's about a mile or so off the north tip of Thetis. Apparently they leased it out to a silver mining operation during the fifties and sixties, but it's deserted now. I found two newspaper stories decrying the deplorable state of the silver mine — the caves and tunnels are in dreadful disrepair. There've been numerous mudslides and cave-ins. Seems the sea is working very hard to stake its claim to the mine. And several spelunkers got lost there and were never found. Serves them right for trespassing, don't you —"

"Francis," I growled.

"Right. Well, that's the Ciel connection."

My mind was racing. "Is that it? All?"

"All?" he asked petulantly. "I thought it was quite a lot. Considering what you gave me to work with."

"Yes, it was a lot," I said patiently. "And as usual you worked miracles. But is there anything else I should know?"

"That's it, dearie," he concluded, mollified.

"Thanks, Francis." I hung up and leaped out of my chair. Thetis, for Christ's sake. If I left now ... The phone rang again, interrupting my plans.

"Yeah?"

"Caitlin, it's Lester."

"Everything okay?"

"Yes. I did the chores. Gray's asleep. She gave me instructions to wake her up every two hours and ask her the day and her name."

"That seems sensible. Listen, kiddo, I have to make a trip up island."

"I know."

"You know? How in hell could you?"

"Well, um, Gray told me. That's what I'm calling you about."

"Oh yeah?"

"I wrote it down because it's so weird. Here's what Gray told me to tell you — to wash a pair of heavy pants, a turtleneck, and underwear. Use no soap. Then dry them without using those dryer thingies. While they're drying, you are to shower without soap or shampoo. Once your clothes are dry, dress without using deodorant or any cologne."

"Lester, is this a joke?"

"No ma'am," he said. "I'm telling you exactly what she told me to. You're to bring a heavy jacket and wear a digital watch with a built-in light. Oh, and bring a flashlight, too."

"Where in hell are we going — a costume party for those with no olfactory nerves?"

"I don't know. Gray said something about caves and tunnels. Then she said that you knew all about it and that I didn't have to know anything about it. All I had to do was drive."

Caves and tunnels? How could Gray know anything about that? I'd talked to Francis about the abandoned silver mine only three minutes ago. This was too weird. "Drive?" I yelled. "No way. You're not going anywhere, buster."

"Don't get excited. She said it would be all right."

"Yeah, well, it isn't all right. And I'll get as excited as I want."

"You're the boss," he said disconsolately. "But Gray said to meet us here just before six."

Maybe I'd better stop in, I thought. It sounded like Gray had wigged out. And really, I wouldn't lose any time. Her place was just a short detour off the highway. Besides, there was nothing to be gained by rushing off in the middle of the night. As I recalled, the ferry to Thetis ran only once a day — just before noon. "I'm not happy about this, Lester," I told him. "I will stop in, but I don't think either of you is going anywhere with me."

"She thinks you need help," he said in a how-can-you-be-so-ungrateful voice.

"I probably do," I informed him, "but I'm not involving a head-injured Asian animal psychologist and an overeager camera shop owner in this mess. One person has already been hurt, remember?" And one person is very likely dead, I thought. No. No way were Gray and Lester going to Ciel with me.

"But what shall I tell Gray?"

"About what?"

"About the clothes-washing and showering and so on."

"Oh for God's sake. Tell her you gave me the message."

"That's all?"

"That's all."

"Okay," he said resignedly. "You know, you have this problem with control."

"Oh I do, do I?" I answered testily. "As I see it, I have no problem at all with control. I'm the one in control and if that's a problem for you, that's too bad."

"That's not what I meant," he said wearily, "and you know it."

" 'Night, Lester," I said just before I hung up.

I paced around the living room pondering Gray's requests. I'd never heard anything so strange. The more I thought about them, the more they sounded suspiciously ritualistic. Oh, what the hell. Even if I got there and discovered she'd become a raving lunatic, I wouldn't have lost much. I could continue on my way and still get to Chemainus in plenty of time for the ferry to Thetis. Heck, in the time I had to spare, I could even buy some deodorant.

Thinking ahead to tomorrow, I filled the cats' kibble dishes to the brim and scribbled a note for Malcolm and Yvonne. This I tacked to the outside of my pantry door — a little insurance policy for the cats in case something dire happened to me. In that unhappy event, at least my furry brood wouldn't starve to death. As an afterthought, I guiltily scribbled a promise to call them about their theft problem as soon as I returned. Then I went in search of a heavy pair of jeans and a nice thick navy turtleneck. I tossed in some already clean underwear, bemoaning the fact that they would soon be indigo, and added a T-shirt and a pair of woolly socks to the load. They all sloshed together happily, sans soap, just as Gray had requested. I stood in the laundry room, hands in my pockets, mind in neutral. Chemainus. Thetis. Ciel. Caves and tunnels. The washer emptied, and I tossed the load into the drier, checking inside first for any of those little wispy white thingies. Nope.

On my way to the shower, I paused, a memory from long ago pricking me. Jonna's grandmother — where was that buckskin bag that she had given me? I thought I knew. A quick check in the little cedar box where I keep my treasures informed me that it was indeed still there. What was it Fleur had told me — that I would know what to do with this when the time came? I suspected the time was just about at hand. And the gift she had spoken of, the gift for Okwaho, the wolf clan — well, I thought I knew what the gift was. It was ten years old and had a gap between its front teeth.

Then I went off to shower. It might have been the nice hot water, or the lateness of the hour, or the excitement of the day, but I could hardly lift my arms to towel myself dry. Sacking out on the bath mat seemed a pretty attractive idea, but I managed somehow to drag myself to bed, set the alarm, and wrap myself in my sheets. My last conscious thoughts were that I should probably tell Tonia where I was going, but as I wasn't really sure of my final destination, I decided not to make the effort. Besides, did this qualify as something she ought to worry about? Who knew? As I tumbled into the black pit of sleep, I thought I heard the clinking of a bell buoy and the *sssss* of spent breakers as they reached their foamy fingers up a pebble beach. But of course, that was ridiculous.

TUESDAY

Chapter 9

The phone rang at five-ten, just as I was headed out the door, and the only reason I picked it up was because I thought it might be Lester.

"What?" I asked gruffly, shrugging into my bomber jacket.

"It's Sandy," the familiar voice said. "Sorry to call so early, but I have to go over to South Van on the six-thirty air taxi."

A lump formed in my throat and I knew before he said so what his reason was for calling. Still, I waited for him to say it.

"It's Jonna. Jory's mother," he added inanely. "South Van found her body earlier this morning."

"Where?" I managed to ask.

"On the beach. About a mile from the motel."

"How can they be sure it's her?"

"She had identification — her driver's license. Other things. I'm sorry," he added.

"Me, too," I said automatically. "What was the cause of death?"

"Unofficially?"

"Yeah. Unofficially."

"A blow to the head with a blunt instrument. Quite a heavy blow. Probably she lost consciousness and never regained it."

"So she couldn't have walked out of the motel on her own and, say, wandered around for two days."

"No."

"It seems that Jory was telling us the truth all along."

"So it seems." He sighed.

I was a whisker away from telling him about Thetis and Ciel and asking for his help — well, it would be the RCMP's help because kidnapping was a federal matter — but a panicked interior voice just wouldn't let me do it. How fast could they move? How many hours would we waste in sitting in hot, smoke-filled offices filling out forms? We needed every hour.

"There's an all-points out on Ratliffe," Sandy told me.

I resisted uttering any one of a number of sarcastic replies that sprang to my lips. "Good," I said noncommittally. Ratliffe was already where he always wanted to be — Heaven. Well, he wasn't going to stay there, not if I had anything to do with it. "Listen, Sandy, thanks for calling, but I gotta run," I said. "Early morning appointment."

"Oh, well, all right." He sounded genuinely contrite. Too bad, I thought as I hung up the phone. Too bloody bad.

On my way to Gray's, I found myself consumed with equal parts rage and guilt. Rage because no one had really given much credence to Jory's account of what had happened to her mother: not Sandy or South Van and, if I was honest with myself, not even me. Even though Jory's version of things was most logical. It was the conversation with Mrs. Andresson that had done it. That and Jory's own admission that she sometimes made up stories. Shit. Why had I found it so difficult to reconcile the fact that a sensitive, intelligent, abused child who made up fantasies to "live in" still might be telling the truth about what her father had done? Why couldn't I accept that even though she made up stories to make her life more bearable, she nonetheless had seen what she said she had? The police had declined to believe her because the absence of a body said to them that no crime had been committed. And I? I had declined to believe her because it suited me. I wanted to believe that Jonna was still alive, that there was still some hope. But now I knew.

Ratliffe. I ground my teeth. What did he have in mind for himself and Jory? Did he think he could just disappear — hole up until everyone had forgotten about him? To hell with that. I was going to see to it that he didn't escape justice that easily. He had laid his long shadow over three lives — Jonna's, Jory's, and mine — and he needed to be called to account for his deeds. I couldn't help what had happened to Jonna, but I figured I had a good crack at salvaging Jory. If I could get there in time.

And then there was the guilt. Jonna was dead and Kirk Ratliffe had killed her and taken the body down to the beach and thrown it off the breakwater. And I would never know what she had wanted to tell me — eleven years ago, when I had just hung up on her, or three days ago, when she had called me for help. It didn't take a genius to figure out that she had called eleven years ago just after Jory was born. What had she wanted to tell me then? Whatever it was, I hadn't wanted to hear it. Whatever it was, I would never know now. And three days ago? "There's something I want you to know," she had said, "and when all this is over, I'll tell you." All this? Poor Jonna — had she really thought it could be "over" without mishap? It seemed as though fate had marked her for tragedy since before I had known her. What was it her grandmother had said — that she had been touched by the Crooked Man? A fanciful thought. Now, from the benefit of years, I saw that she had been a victim, nothing more poetic than that. Could I have helped her eleven years ago? Probably. If I hadn't been so righteously indignant. Hey, she'd done me wrong, and in the best country-and-western song tradition, was I going to let her tromp on my heart again? Nosiree. So I'd just hung up, before she had a chance to ask me for anything. Atta girl, Caitlin.

And three days ago? Why had I talked to her then? God, who knows? Maybe I was eleven years wiser or mellower. Maybe I was just curious. Whatever the reason, I *had* listened to her. And talked. And yes, it had wrenched my heart to hear her voice, goddamit. And, finally, I had to admit that that was what I had been fleeing all these years. Having my heart wrenched, my feelings tromped on. Because I *had* loved her. Foolish or not, inappropriate or not, I had loved her.

"Yes, goddamit!" I yelled to the tag-end of night, through which I saw myself flying like some dark avenging angel, like destiny's black arrow. "I loved you!" And these words, which I had not permitted myself to say or think for twenty-two years, seemed to tear something loose inside me. It started as an intolerable feeling of fullness just below my heart and rose rapidly until I was choking on it, on this something that had to be released. I opened my mouth and shrieked like an animal in pain. "I loved you!" I screamed, driving my car into the deserted parking lot of the Donut Stop, braking savagely. "I loved you, you shit, you goddamned whore, you know-nothing bitch ... you, you ... Why couldn't you have loved me back?"

Unable to think of additional imprecations, I just wept, leaning my head on the steering wheel, howling like a kicked dog until at last I was cried out. "Ah, Jonna. Why?" I said, wiping my nose on a handful of napkins I found in the glove compartment. Good show, Caitlin, I said to myself. Cry a little, why don't you. Behave like a teenager. Heterosexuals learn these lessons when they're fifteen. You're forty. This is, to say the least, puerile. Get a grip. So she didn't love you back. So what? She wasn't worth it anyhow.

Yeah, I thought, navigating my way back onto the highway, so what? I'd lived. Yes indeedy. But I knew the price I'd paid. Once bitten, twice shy — wasn't that the old saw? I'm a quick study, and what I learned from that little bit of pathos was that those warm fuzzy feelings I experienced for people to whom I was attracted were usually lust, not love. Indeed, not one of the ladies with whom I had dallied had ever heard the L word from my lips. For that matter, I'd never heard it from theirs either. Was I missing something? Hell. Who knew? Lust was nice and tidy. Predictable. Short-lived. Love was . . . something else.

Giving my nose a final blow, I turned off Saanich Highway onto the little lane that led to Gray's place.

They were waiting for me, Gray and Lester, in Lester's jeep.

"You're late," he informed me. "We wondered if you'd had . . . trouble."

I thought of the half hour I'd spent blubbering in the Donut Stop's parking lot and hoped it wasn't time I'd regret. "Yeah, I had trouble. This whole case has been trouble. And I'm keeping you out of it. You aren't going anywhere."

"But —" he protested.

"Forget it," I said as authoritatively as I could. "You don't know one quarter of what I know about what's waiting up-island. Believe me, you're not going." I poked my head into the back of the jeep where Gray's face was a pale blur in the half-light, her white bandage a testament to how this case had spilled over and touched others. "Neither are you," I told her. "I can manage this by myself."

"No, you cannot," Gray said softly. "You need both of us to help you. Please get in. Time is growing short."

"Wait a minute here," I said, feeling like a stampeded horse. "This is *my* case. These are *my* problems."

"Not completely," Gray said.

"Please, Gray. Be straight with me," I told her wearily. "No semantic games."

"Very well. You cannot manage this alone. You know nothing about caves and tunnels and how to track people through them. I do."

"You do?"

"I do. I will tell you all about that later."

I was tired of being put off. "No. Tell me now."

She gave me a flat, dark-eyed look. "When I was unconscious in the hospital, I had what you would call a dream."

"What I would call a dream — what would you call it?"

"A memory of the future."

I ground my teeth in frustration. "So, what did you dream?"

"I dreamed of interconnecting caves and smaller tunnels leading off them. I was there for days it seemed, by myself, searching. And then I came to a place I knew. I saw people I had not seen for many years and everything was familiar to me. I felt ... at home. There was a great sense of peace. In my dream, I slept, and in my sleep I heard your voice calling me from very far off. And as though your voice had opened up a channel to something, a terrible sense of menace came along with your voice, like an odor. I resisted replying, but the menace was . . . shrill, like a sound rising in pitch so that I could not ignore it. So I spoke your name to warn you, and all at once I was . . . where I had been. Back in the hospital room."

I swallowed. "Is that when you said 'Caitlin,' and sat up? Lester told me."

"Yes."

I didn't know what to say. Questions swarmed in my head like bees. "Gray _"

"There is no time now for questions," she said. "Now we must hurry. Later, there will be time."

I shrugged. There was nothing left now but to trust her. "Get in," I told Lester. "Drive."

"Okay," he said, sounding eager and grateful all at once. "But, er, where?"

"Chemainus," I told him. "And step on it. We have to catch the ferry to Thetis." I put my gear in the back beside Gray and sat in the front seat next to Lester. A terrible weariness had suddenly come over me. "Who knows where you're going?" I asked him.

"I left a message for Doreen at the camera shop. She's going to mind the store. She'll come by and feed Gray's animals too."

"Such foresight," I said to him. "Did you two cook this up last night?"

"Well, we talked about it," he said defensively.

"Hmmm." I looked back over my shoulder, but Gray was staring into the middle distance, not asleep, but not exactly awake and with us, either. What was she seeing? "I'm going to have a snooze,"

I told him. "Check every so often to see that Gray isn't asleep. Her head," I reminded him.

"Righto," he agreed happily.

Jesus — would he ever stop thinking that what I did was exciting and glamorous? Righto indeed. I snuggled down into the collar of my bomber jacket and dozed off.

Where was I? How did I get down here? Had my mother sent me down to the pantry for a jar of the pickles she stored there? I couldn't remember, but I knew that I had such a dread of small, dark spaces that I couldn't imagine what had possessed me to come down to the cellar by myself. Opening my eyes very wide, I tried to see something, anything, in the gloom. Nothing. Where was the bloody light switch? Well, maybe it didn't matter that much. There was a light just inside the pantry door. All I had to do was walk straight ahead. I thrust my arms out in front of me and walked forward ... into a cold, hard, rocklike surface. What the hell? I ran my hands over the wall I'd walked into, searching for the pantry door, but the rock or whatever it was, was seamless. This was crazy, I decided. There wasn't such a wall in our basement. Except for the pantry door, which was made of planks of unfinished pine, the basement walls were paneled. Not so these. With my palms against the wall, I slid fifty paces to my right. Nothing changed. The surface was irregular and bumpy under my fingers — it reminded me of a cliff face I had scaled once. But something was very wrong — our basement was not fifty paces long. My heart bumped alarmingly in my chest. Where was the pantry door?

"Caitlinnnn." The sound was so faint that at first I thought I had imagined it. It seemed to be coming from ahead of me. I held my breath and listened. "Caitlinnnn." Dammit, it *wasn't* my imagination. It was louder this time, and now it was accompanied by a rustle as though someone was walking slowly, deliberately through dead leaves. I swallowed. Someone who knew my name was coming my way, out of the darkness. I suddenly decided I did not want to meet this someone. Dropping to a crouch, I half-walked, half-ran back the way I had come. I was not panicking, I told myself, I was simply retreating. But when I had retreated fifty paces, I stopped. Now what?

"Caitlinnnn," the voice called, a whispery, mournful appeal. The bottom fell out of my stomach and I turned in headlong flight ... and ran into the basement stairs, cracking my ankles, elbows, and knees as I fell full length onto the unforgiving wood. My eyes teared from the sharp flares of agony but I got my feet underneath me and looked up. Light! A faint rectangular frame of gray — light seeping through the cracks around the basement door! With a cry, I bounded up one stair ... but something seized me by the ankle and pulled me back.

"Caitlinnnn," the voice moaned at my feet. In a frenzy of terror, I kicked and twisted, but the thing held me fast.

"No!" Lashing out savagely, I felt my foot connect with something soft ... and came yelling awake in Lester's jeep.

"Jeez!" he said. "That must've been some dream. Are you all right?"

Dazed, I looked around. Was I all right? My knee hurt like hell where I guessed I had tried to drop-kick Lester's glove compartment and my pulse was about two hundred. But other than that I seemed unharmed. "Yeah," I said wearily. "I'm all right."

"What was it?" he asked, concerned.

"Nothing . . . real. A nightmare from my past."

"Oh," he said and relaxed.

I scrubbed my hands over my face and through my hair. "I'd like some coffee," I announced. "What about you, kiddo?"

He looked at his watch. "We're doing okay. We should get there with plenty of time to spare. Let's see . . . Mill Bay is coming up. We could stop there."

"Fine," I told him. A quick look over my shoulder showed me Gray surreptitiously fingering her bandage. "Does it hurt?" I asked her.

She smiled, a rueful grin that turned her mouth down at the corners. "No."

Liar, I thought as I nodded dutifully, turning around. What a sad excuse for the calvary we were.

I settled back into Lester's uncomfortable passenger seat and crossed my arms, brooding. What I had told him was not exactly true. The figure that pursued me through my dreams was not a nightmare from the past — it was an entity that I had come to know well, one of a pair of gifts from the Llewelyns, my mother's side of our family. All the Llewelyn women are a little strange — two of my aunts were certifiably nuts. And me? What I got along with the Llewelyn's Celtic genes was a rudimentary kind of clairvoyance. Sometimes, when I'm under stress, my brain just seems to kick into another gear and I suddenly *know* things. I can't explain it any other way. My other gift (ha!) from my mother's clan is the Dark Lady.

My Aunt Fiona saw a lot of the Dark Lady in the year before her death. In fact, Aunt Fee used to sit on a chair at the top of the cellar stairs and wait for the Dark Lady to come get her. Was I going to go the way of Auntie Fee? Not if I could help it. I'd made an uneasy accommodation with that spectral presence, for I'd made her acquaintance often enough in dreamtime to know what her appearance presaged. It was a warning, plain and simple, a message from whatever goddess still watched over the Llewelyns, a sign that said BE CAREFUL. I'd never discussed this with anyone, but I knew from experience that the appearance of the Dark Lady in my dreams meant that I'd bloody well better watch out.

"How's this?" Lester asked as we pulled into the nearly deserted parking lot of a little coffee shop. Gold ropes of tinsel snaked their way across the front of the building, and a garish MERRY CHRISTMAS painted in red and green on the big front window served to remind us that so-called festive season was well advanced.

"Bah, humbug," I told him, slapping a five dollar bill into his hand. "Coffee for me. Black. And something to raise my blood sugar. A couple of donuts, say. Get yourself some tea. Gray? Want something?"

"Perhaps some tea," she replied.

As Lester went into the coffee shop, I got out

and walked across the parking lot to a little fringe of cedars through which I could see the ocean. Just beyond the trees a six-foot bank fell steeply to the water and I stood on the edge, hands in my pockets, looking out to sea. A gusty wind blew across the water and I noted with dismay that a three- or four-foot swell was breaking against the headland just to the north. Here it was a little more protected, but out on the open ocean conditions did not look good. How rough would it have to be for the ferry to stop running, I wondered. A strong, wet gust of wind rocked me back onto my heels, and I touched my lips with my tongue, tasting salt. Damnation. There was quite a storm brewing out there.

Lester came up behind me. "Doesn't look good, does it?" he asked, blue eyes worried behind his glasses. "What'll we do if we ... you know, if the ferry stops running?"

I shrugged. "Rent a boat. Swim." I saw the horror in his eyes and realized that I ought not to be so literal with him. Poor kid — he believed what I told him. I patted his shoulder. "Let's not waste energy worrying. We'll make haste to the ferry dock and worry then if we have to."

"Okay," he said unhappily.

I put an arm around his shoulders. "It's not your problem you know," I said softly. "You're just the driver, remember?"

"Yeah," he said. "Not that you two would ever tell a guy anything, but I think I know what's happening."

"Oh you do, do you, Mr. Sleuth? Just what do you think is happening?"

"Well, you and Gray are after the creep who slugged her. Ratliffe. He kidnapped his daughter. He's some kind of pervert."

"Give the man a cigar," I said softly.

He blushed. "So I know it's important that we get over to Thetis. And I know you'll do something ... extreme if you find you can't. I just thought I'd do a little worrying ahead of time."

I ruffled his hair. "Why not? Let's go drink that coffee and tea you bought and boogie on down the road to Chemainus. If we're in luck we'll be able to board the ferry. If not ..." I shrugged.

"Then what?" he asked.

"Then we go to Plan B."

"I hate your Plan Bs."

"I didn't ask you to come, junior. You could be at home toasting your toes in front of your very own fireplace, drinking wassail, and putting the finishing touches on your presents. Instead you're freezing your buns off in a force nine gale playing chauffeur to an Asian witch and a Celtic numbskull who meddles in other people's business. Not a great way to celebrate Christmas."

"I know," he said wearily. "I was the one who wanted to come."

"Indeed you were," I told him frostily. "So let's get to where we're going, get the dirty deed done, and get on home so you can roast your chestnuts."

"Okay," he said, sighing.

"You betcha," I said, walking him back to the jeep, an arm around his shoulders. But I'd heard the edge of doubt in his voice. For that matter, what *did* I intend to do if I got to Chemainus and found there was no ferry? Well that depended on where Ratliffe and Jory were. If they were already on Thetis or, worse yet, on Ciel, I'd just have to think of a way to get there too. I slammed the jeep's door and, fiddling with my coffee, said a silent prayer that the ferry would still be running. Because my Plan B was nonexistent.

Chapter 10

Just past Mill Bay, the highway turns inland through pine and fir forests, protecting travelers from the worst of the weather. For this small mercy, I was grateful. In an eerie limbo of near-calm, Lester's jeep sped down a gloomy green corridor like a bullet hurtling down the barrel of a gun. The only indication of the building storm was an occasional gust of wind that whipped the treetops nearly horizontal. I eyed the darkening sky nervously, and sure enough, once we turned east again, parallel to the ocean, the trees thinned and the storm hit us like a fist.

"Hey!" Lester exclaimed, fighting to dissuade the jeep from heading for the shoulder of the road.

I looked out to sea. Against the eastern horizon, the hilly bulk of Saltspring Island loomed like a breaching sea monster. Almost dead ahead rose the tantalizingly close green-forested slopes of Kuper and Thetis Islands with their calm harbors and safe inlets. But between us and them lay the waters of Stuart Channel. And right at the moment, it looked as though a giant Cuisinart were at work here. I couldn't even imagine taking a boat out in that tossing maelstrom. "Shit!" I yelled. As if in perverse response, the wind howled in a minor key, smacking the jeep another buffet. I realized we'd be lucky to make it to town.

We almost didn't. Lester wrestled the wheel all the way into Chemainus and we reached the outskirts of the village with something like twenty minutes to spare.

"Hey, it looks like they're loading!" Lester exclaimed as we topped a little rise. From our vantage point we could see across the roofs of the little town to the ferry docks where a very short line of cars was indeed making its way onto the top deck of a green and white B.C. ferry.

"I guess they know what they're doing," I said. "God, I hope they sell Dramamine on board."

We pulled up at the dock just as the silver van ahead of us drove up the ramp and onto the top deck. One of the ferry crew — a young guy in a two-piece yellow rubber rainsuit, scuffed boots, and a green stocking cap pulled down to his eyes — motioned for Lester to roll down the window.

"The captain says we'll make it to Thetis all right, but the ferry is going to have to stay there until the weather breaks," he told us through chattering teeth. "Maybe three or four days. If you still want to make the crossing, you can pay at the Purser's Office. We need to cast off."

Lester looked over at me uncertainly. "We want to make the crossing," I told the crewman.

He shrugged. "It's up to you. Drive straight up the ramp," he told Lester. "Someone will show you where to park. Be sure to leave the brake on. And be careful when you get out. It's damned windy up there. Slippery, too."

We parked behind the silver van and cautiously opened the jeep's doors. A succession of gusts buffeted our ears and plucked at our clothing as we ran for the stairway to the enclosed lower deck. To the banshee wailing of the gale, we fell through the doorway.

"Holy mackerel, what a storm!" Lester said as the wind blew us through the door. "Are you sure the captain knows what he's doing?"

"Beats me," I told him. "Why don't you two see if there's anything to eat. I'll go find the Purser's Office."

I left Lester and Gray making their way toward the canteen at the other end of the passenger lounge. A sign marked CREW seemed to indicate that I might find the Purser at the opposite end of the boat, so I staggered between tables that were completely empty save for a party of four men in one corner, smoking and reading newspapers, and two couples snoozing. An arrow directed me around the corner and down a little companionway and as the ferry gave a lurch, I stumbled into the Dutch door that said PURSER, feeling like an ass.

"Quite a blow," said a voice behind me. I turned around. The young guy I had seen earlier was peeling off his rainsuit, stepping out of boots and yellow rubber pants unselfconsciously, pulling off his jacket. "Excuse me," he said, reaching past me to hang things up. The last thing to go was the green stocking cap and when he pulled that off, shaking out a mane of crisply curling blond hair, I realized that this crew member was a young woman. As she opened the door to the Purser's Office and stepped inside, I had a chance to admire her well-tailored navy pants and heavy white wool turtleneck with navy epaulets. A name tag just above one breast said POLLY TRIVERS — PURSER. Ah, the appeal of a woman in uniform.

"Omigosh!" she said, sneezing into a hastily grabbed handful of Kleenex.

"Bless you," I replied. "Are we really going to make it to Thetis?"

"Sure," she said, giving me a grin. "We've made the crossing in worse storms than this. Besides, the wind's with us. Are you paying for the jeep?"

"Yeah. And three passengers."

She took my money and counted out change.

"What do you do for three or four days on Thetis when you end up stranded there?" I asked her.

"Oh, this and that. I can stay in my parents'

177

house so it's no big deal. The others put up in the local hotel, play some cards. I catch up on my sleep." She gave me an appraising look and a smile that curled my toes. "Where are you folks staying?"

I forced myself to ignore the smile. "We're not. We need to get on over to Ciel."

She raised her pale eyebrows. "Ciel? No one will take you over to Ciel in this weather. You'll just have to wait."

"We'll see," I said, not wanting to give up.

"I'm not kidding," she said, shaking her head emphatically. "I know all the locals and none of them will put out in a storm like this. It's only a mile and a half, but nobody's that daft."

"Tell me something," I said. "Did you make this run yesterday?"

"Uh huh."

"Was it crowded?"

"Nope. Never is this time of year."

"Maybe you noticed a man in his early forties, and a little girl with dark hair, probably braided? He would have been driving a car with Ontario plates."

"Yeah. Why do you want to know?"

I ran a hand through my hair. What the hell, sometimes telling the truth was the wisest course of action. "He's a child molester. The girl is his daughter. He almost killed my friend when he kidnapped the kid. I'm a private detective hired to get her back."

Her eyebrows shot up. "Really? And he's there? On Thetis?"

"Depends on the weather. Could he have gotten off Thetis yesterday?"

"Oh sure. There was just a little wind. Nothing like this."

"Then they're over on Ciel. That's where he planned to take her."

"Are you sure? Ciel is a privately owned island. There's nothing there except an old mine and a couple of rundown summer places."

"Right. His family owns them."

"Oooh. Then he's a Ratliffe."

"Yeah. He sure enough is."

Some of the frustration and rage I was feeling must have leaked through into my voice, because Polly gave me a searching look. "Why aren't the police involved in this?" she asked.

I laughed bitterly. "They are — about three days too late. The South Van force wouldn't believe Jory — that's Ratliffe's daughter — when she told them she'd seen him kill her mother. No body, you see. That kind of ruined her credibility with the law. So even if she'd been tempted to tell them that dear old dad had been molesting her and had plans to run off with her to his ancestral island, do you think they'd have even been interested? Fat chance. They diddled around just long enough to give him a chance to snatch her." I snorted. "I'll call the police once I have Jory safe and her dad tied to the nearest fir."

"I'm afraid I'd do more than that to him," she said.

"Yeah, well, I worry about that sometimes too."

"Let me help," she offered after a moment of lip-chewing.

I raised an eyebrow. "What do you have in mind?"

"Let's find out if he did get over to Ciel. I'll call the little marina on the east side of the island. If anyone took him over, they did."

"Okay," I said, surprised at her generosity.

"This'll take a few minutes. Why don't you go grab some coffee. The galley is back around the corner."

"Yeah, I saw it earlier. Want some?"

"Sure. Black with sugar, please," she called over her shoulder, bending to adjust the dials on a radio set.

I hustled in the direction of the galley, grabbing onto tables occasionally as the ferry bucked and lurched in the gale. Lester and Gray were at a table by the window, reading newspapers. I bought two paper cups of coffee and carried them back toward the Purser's Office.

"Bad news," Polly told me as I handed her coffee across the Dutch doors. "Arthur at Snug Harbor took them across yesterday."

I was too disappointed even to curse.

"Listen, we're about to dock," she said. "I have to go direct traffic. Why don't you folks check into the hotel and I'll meet you in the bar in, say, an hour. I've got an idea, but ... well, I have to do some checking first."

I tried not to get my hopes up. What the hell — if her idea didn't pan out, I was no further behind. It wasn't as if I had any ideas of my own. Maybe I'd get drunk — I hadn't done that for years. At least I wouldn't have to drive anywhere — I could just fall out of my chair at the bar and they could drag me upstairs. "You're on," I told her, and prepared to go get Lester and Gray.

"Wait," she called.

I turned. "Yeah?"

"Well, I ... it just occurred to me, I don't even know your name."

"Reece," I told her. "Caitlin Reece."

Any other time, the approach to Thetis would have been something to rhapsodize about. I'm sure the little horseshoe-shaped harbor would have been postcard-pretty when the jade waters were calm and the robin's-egg blue sky was dotted with fluffy clouds. Now, however, we sat in our vehicles, gnawing our fingernails as the captain took dead aim at the harbor entrance, gave the engines a final burst of power, and flung us through the open end of the horseshoe. I closed my eyes, praying we wouldn't kiss the cliffs that loomed uncomfortably close to my side of the ferry.

"Oh, jeez," Lester sighed as we spurted into the calmer waters of the harbor like a cork popped from a champagne bottle.

"My thoughts exactly," I told him, feeling my heart rate drop by about fifty beats.

We clunked and clanked up against the ferry dock and when we were finally made fast, a yellow-rainsuited figure stood on the dock, waving traffic ashore — all five cars.

"Straight ahead to the hotel," I told Lester. "Apparently it's on the main drag and there's only one."

By the time we parked and ran up the steps of the hotel, a miserable, cold rain had started. My

VISA card was good enough to get us three adjoining rooms and the white-haired woman at the front desk informed us that they'd soon be lighting the fire in the bar, where they'd be serving lunch.

"It'll only be soup and sandwiches this time of year," she apologized. "We do better at supper. There's a pharmacy just down the street," she said. "For toothbrushes and so on." Plainly she'd had to play hostess to plenty of stranded travelers.

"I'm working on Plan B," I told Lester. Gray had gone upstairs ahead of us and we followed slowly through a little library toward the broad green-carpeted staircase. I put a hand on his arm. "Take care of Gray, will you? And maybe find out if there's a doctor in town in case we need someone to look at her head in the middle of the night."

"Okay. She seems fine, though," he said. "We were talking on the ferry and she's coherent and everything."

"Good. Let's just make sure she stays that way."

"I guess we're not going anywhere for a few days, are we?"

"You never know," I told him. "Like I said, I'm working on something. I'll let you know when it comes together."

"I'll ask Gray what she needs and make a run to the pharmacy. Then we'll probably have lunch."

"Okay. Just make sure I can find you." My mind was already on my meeting with Polly. "Gotta go. I'll check back with you soon, Lester."

* * * * *

Polly was waiting for me at a table in the corner of the bar. Sure enough, someone had lit the fire in the huge stone fireplace and it popped and crackled merrily, orange tongues of flame caressing logs that must have been four feet long. Another time I would have been entranced; now, I was too anxious and frustrated to be appreciative. I took a chair across the table from Polly.

"Caitlin, hi," she said, looking up from her sandwich and beer. "Want something?"

"Oh, maybe a sandwich. What's on the menu?"

"They'll make you anything you like, within reason. This is egg salad."

"That'll do. And some coffee."

Polly waved and a young redheaded guy with a towel tucked into the waistband of his jeans came hurrying over.

"Hi, Pol," he said shyly, evidently smitten with her. I couldn't blame him.

"Another sandwich, Angus, and some coffee," she told him. He wrote the order down carefully and hurried away.

"I'm waiting for a phone call," she said. "When it comes, I may be able to help you. Let's talk about something else in the meantime. I don't want to jinx things."

"Okay," I said, mystified. "So, tell me, how does a nice girl like you get to be a purser for B.C. Ferries?"

She laughed and I noticed what even white teeth she had. Gosh, she might be all of twenty-five. "Well, I love the sea but I didn't have the guts to go work on the salmon boats. I figured the ferry system would be a good compromise."

"Don't you get bored seeing the same old scenery?"

She shook her head. "Nope. We're assigned to different runs. I like this one best, though. It's like coming home. I used to live here," she explained.

"Used to?"

"Yeah. I live on Saltspring now. My parents' house is here, but I ..." She looked away. "When they died, I moved out. I rent the place out in summers to tourists. And I stay there when I'm stranded. Like now. But I don't want to live there."

I was willing to bet there was something more to that little story, but I nodded. "Saltspring is nice," I said blandly.

"Yeah," she replied, looking into the fire. "So tell me about yourself," she asked, a little too brightly.

"Gosh, ma'am," I said, trying to lighten the mood, "there's not much to tell. I used to work in the Crown Prosecutor's office but I got tired of that. So I went into business for myself. Now I help out people the system can't." I shrugged. "That's it."

"Who hired you for this job? A relative?"

I decided to tell her the truth, or most of it, anyhow. "No. Jory hired me."

"Jory? The little girl?" She was plainly astonished.

"Mmmhmm."

"What did she want you to do?"

"To find her father and hand him over to the police."

"Wow. How did she know to come to you?"

"Her mother and I have, had ... old history between us."

Comprehension dawned in her eyes. "Oh."

Fortunately the egg sandwich and coffee arrived at that moment, making further conversation unnecessary.

"Phone for you, Pol," Angus told her. "Dad said you can take it in his office."

While Polly was gone, I polished off the sandwich and coffee, then sat back, looking around the bar. The quartet from the ferry was ensconced at a large table by the window, looking gloomy. Two other tables were taken up by locals. I tried to will myself into calm, telling myself there wasn't a thing in hell I could do to help Jory, but it wasn't working. I shredded my napkin and had started on a troublesome hangnail when Polly reappeared, looking flushed.

"Here's the deal. I called my friend Mel at the meteorological office. He read the satellite picture for me. There's going to be a break in this storm sometime before morning. But it won't be a very big break — maybe six hours, he says. Then another storm is due in. So ... if you still want to get over to Ciel —"

"Do I? Yeah, I do. Where can I get a boat?"

She shook her head. "No one would rent you a boat. Or take you over. It's too risky." She took a deep breath. "But I will. My dad's Boston Whaler is in the boathouse at my parents' place. I had it out two weeks ago, so I know it's running okay. All I need to do is check it over."

"Polly, don't think I'm unappreciative, but why in hell would you do this? You said yourself it's risky."

She looked down at her clasped hands. "I ... when I think of that little girl, taken by *her own father*, someone she ought to be able to trust, I ... well, it just makes me want to do whatever I can to help," she finished lamely.

Now I understood the ambivalence she had expressed about her parents' house. Her father's house. Jesus. Maggie Kent had told me that probably one out of every three girls were the victims of child molesters. But how many of those molesters had been their own *fathers*? I wanted to throw up. "Okay. I'll take your help," I told her. "Now what?"

"Now we get on over to the other side of the island before the road floods out. I'll check over the Whaler, then we wait for the break in the weather. Do you want to tell your friends?"

For one instant I was tempted just to walk away, to go with Polly, to get this thing done and not involve Lester and Gray. But I couldn't do that. Lester had guilt he needed to expiate by being useful. And Gray? Gray was convinced she needed to come with me. Who was I to argue? "Yeah. I'll tell them."

"Hey, this is some neat place!" Lester exclaimed as we followed Polly's yellow VW Bug into the carport. A big, two-story home faced with natural rock, Polly's house was set well back from the road, behind a holly hedge, on about an acre of well-tended lawn. Behind the house I could see the ocean, and about a mile out to sea, through a curtain of rain, the dark blur of Ciel. I ground my teeth in frustration — so near.

Polly hurried up the front steps ahead of us and as we huddled under the porch overhang, she struggled with the door.

"Got it!" she exclaimed. "C'mon in. I'll turn the heat on."

Lester, Gray, and I waited in the middle of the living room as Polly raced down to the basement.

"Why's she helping us?" Lester asked in a stage whisper. "Should we trust her? What's in this for her?"

"She's helping because she's a nice person," I told him. "As for whether we should trust her, what other options do we have?"

"Is this Plan B?" he wanted to know.

"Yeah. Got any better ideas?"

He shook his head. "Not a one."

Polly emerged from the basement, wiping her hands on a rag. "There's a guest bedroom and the library down here," she told us. "Upstairs there's my room and my . . . and another bedroom. It'll be hours before we can make the crossing. You could get some sleep if you like. I'll wake you. There's plenty of canned food in the pantry and the gas is on if you want to cook. I'm going to change and then go on down to the boathouse to see about the Whaler. Make yourselves at home."

"Thanks," Lester said. "I think I'll sack out in the library."

Gray gave me an appraising look, then followed Lester.

"Your friend," Polly said, "is she okay? She didn't say a word."

"She's the one Ratliffe clobbered when he snatched Jory," I told her. "I'm sure she has the world's worst headache. I wouldn't want to talk either if I were her. But even when she doesn't have a headache, she's not what you'd call chatty."

"Oh. Well, I'm sure she's very nice."

I burst out laughing. "Gray? No, she's not. But that's okay, Polly."

She looked at me uncertainly. "Do you want ... my parents' bedroom is upstairs and I thought —"

"Sure. I can sack out there. Show me the way."

I followed Polly upstairs and she stopped on the landing. In the light that came through a lace-curtained hall window, I could see that her eyes were troubled. "I used to know him," Polly said faintly. "Kirk Ratliffe. When I was ten or eleven, I used to sail over to Ciel and picnic in the little cove where the bell buoy is. The summer I got my sailboat, he was there with his family. The rumor was he had gotten into trouble back east and the family had brought him here for a few months until things cooled down. He was a grownup, you know — a lot older than me." I winced. Yeah, a lot older. Hell, he was my age. "I used to see him sometimes in town. At the hotel. Around. But he always gave me such weird looks. I was afraid to go ashore when he was there. And he was almost always in the cove, working on their dock. So I tied up at the bell buoy and ate my sandwiches on my boat. He gave me the creeps," she said in a hushed voice. "Now I understand why."

"Smart girl," I said. "He gave me the creeps, too."

"You knew him?"

"Yeah. We were seniors in high school together. Kirk, Jory's mother, and me."

I could see her digesting this. "Oh." After a moment, she said, "So this is sort of a matter of honor for you, isn't it?"

That surprised me because I'd been thinking it was a matter of guilt — something I owed Jonna and something I owed Jory. Honor? I didn't know, but it certainly sounded better. "Maybe so."

She looked at me strangely. "I think I'll change and go check the boat over." Without another word, she walked away.

I shrugged, then let myself into her parents' room. It was dwarfed by an enormous four-poster double bed with a white chenille spread. There were white lace curtains on the windows and on the wood floor were several braided throw rugs. Very country, I thought. On a massive cherrywood dresser sat six silver photo frames — every one turned face down. Curious, I crossed the room and one after another, picked them up. In every picture was a beefy man with curly pale hair, an aggressive chin, and a smile that never did quite reach his eyes. Dad, I supposed. There were two pictures of Dad with Mom — an attractive brunette with a radiant smile — two of Mom and Dad with little Polly, and two of Dad with bigger Polly. Polly's smile, I noted, was nonexistent in the last two pictures. With a sigh, I turned the frames face down again, crossed to the bed and, taking off my shoes, wrapped myself in the bedspread.

* * * * *

I awoke to darkness, carried out of dreams on the crest of a tide of panic. Where in hell was I? What day was it? What was I supposed to be doing? Then I remembered — it was Tuesday. I was in Polly's parents' bedroom. On Thetis. Jesus. I closed my eyes, feeling like a leaf caught up in a whirlpool. For a person who liked very much to be the mistress of her fate, I realized just how little control I had been able to exert over this whole mess. I hadn't acted; I had reacted. Events had just *happened* and, like a bicycle racer, I had drafted off them, carried along in their wake. What if Polly hadn't come along? What if there wasn't a break in the storm? What if, what if. And while I was at it, what if I got to Ciel and found out that Ratliffe had either killed Jory or done something so horrible to her that she'd be beyond help?

I flung off the bedspread and sat up, feeling thick-headed and testy. Pressing the button on my digital watch, I saw that the time was just before midnight. My stomach growled. Time for supper. I decided to creep downstairs and see about that canned food Polly had assured us was in plentiful supply in the pantry. Perhaps it wouldn't be too toxic.

I navigated the stairs, fumbled on the wall for the light to the kitchen, snapped it on, and was halfway to the pantry when I realized someone was sitting at the kitchen table.

"Polly! Jesus, you about gave me a heart attack."

"Sorry," she said sheepishly. "I like to sit here in the dark and look out over the bay." She had changed into jeans and a pink turtleneck and now looked about sixteen. "I realize normal people would turn the light on, but ..." She shrugged.

"But then you wouldn't be able to see the moon rise over Ciel," I said. "Besides, what's so great about being normal?" I poked around in the pantry and found a can of vegetarian chili that didn't look too bad. "Want some?"

"Sure." Polly took the can from me, opened it, and dumped it into a pot.

"Get the boat checked out?"

"Yeah. It's all ready to go."

We sat across the table from each other in what I realized was an extremely awkward silence. Something had happened in the few hours since I'd last seen her. I wondered what. "Penny for your thoughts," I said.

"What? Oh, sorry."

"Listen, if you've changed your mind —" Please, I thought. Please don't have changed your mind.

"No! I haven't. It's not that. It's ... this house."

I thought I understood. "Ghosts?"

"Yeah." The chili had begun to sizzle in the pot and Polly got up to stir it. "I really should sell it. Every time I come back here, I just get all maudlin and depressed."

"Selling might not be a bad idea," I told her softly. "Sometimes we have to cut ourselves off from things that hurt us. Bury them. Let them go." Ha — I should talk.

She nodded. "I know. And not coming here would make it all a whole lot easier."

I hunted around in a cupboard and found a couple of bowls. While Polly dished out the chili, I opened a Labatt's Blue that I found in the fridge. "You're driving," I told her. "No booze. Let's see. There's mineral water or Diet Coke."

"Diet Coke."

We ate in a more comfortable silence now that she had said what was on her mind, and I decided I'd encourage her to talk some more. "Where did you go to school when you lived here?"

"Saltspring. I'd take my bike onto the ferry and pedal to school. I have great memories of that." She chased a bite of chili around her bowl. "Tell me, what's going to happen when we get to Ciel? Do you have, well, a plan?"

I almost laughed out loud. Another youngster who wanted to know what my plans were. "Sort of," I told her. "I'll find Kirk Ratliffe and ask him to hand Jory over to me."

She looked skeptical. "Just like that? He won't give her to you, you know."

"Then I'll just have to take her away from him."

She looked at me searchingly, blue eyes seeking an answer to some question she had yet to ask. I had a feeling it was coming, though. "What if, well, what if he won't let you?"

"Won't let me what? Take her?"

Her eyes were unnaturally bright, and two spots of color had appeared high on her cheekbones. "Yes. What if he says 'No, you can't have her. She's mine to do with as I please. I'm her father. This is none of your business.' "

"Oh I'm sure he will say that, or some variation of it. But it doesn't matter what he says. I'm not leaving Ciel without Jory."

"How?" she asked, eyes brimming with tears. One

192

spilled over and trickled down her cheek. "How will you take her away from him? He's ... a *man*! And he's her father. He's got rights."

"Rights? He has no rights anymore," I said. "He gave those up when he started crawling into bed with his daughter. And as for him being a man, well la-di-da. Men listen very attentively when my .357 talks to them. It's quite an effective conversationalist."

"You really can do it, can't you?" she asked, hope in her voice. "You can take her away from him. You're not afraid."

"Yeah, I can take her away from him. But I never said I wasn't afraid. That doesn't have anything to do with it."

"I don't understand," she said, wiping her eyes with the back of her hand.

I sighed. "It's okay. Sometimes I don't either."

"But if you're afraid —"

"I don't let my self think about it," I told her honestly. "If I did, it would paralyze me. I just do what I have to."

"What you have to? But how do you know what that is?"

I shrugged. "I usually end up doing whatever's necessary to solve the messes my clients get themselves into."

"Including taking the law into your own hands?"

"Sometimes."

She was silent a moment, digesting all this. "I never knew women could do that," she said. "I guess ... I guess I've just never met one who could."

"It's not could," I told her. "It's would."

"I don't understand."

"Look, anyone can learn how to shoot or fight dirty. You need to have something else to go along with it."

"Yeah, guts," she said ruefully.

"No, I don't think so. I think it's ... a determination. You have to reach a point where you say no. And after you say no, everything else is possible. Reaching that point, though, well, that's the hard part."

Her blue eyes filled with tears again. "Where were you fifteen years ago?" she said, misery in her voice. "I'm glad Jory has you on her side, but why wasn't there a Caitlin Reece for me?"

"Oh, sweetie," I said, reaching across the table and taking her hands in mine. "I'm sorry."

"I'm helping you because of what my father did to me," she said, tears streaming down her face.

"I thought so," I told her gently. So she'd finally said it. I thought she would. "The pictures upstairs ..."

"Yes. Those lying pictures. The happy family." She gripped my hands tightly. "I ... I've never told anyone about what happened. It's like it's this private shameful thing that I'm carrying inside me. And it never goes away. I really, really feel sorry for that little girl. Oh, Caitlin, you have to get her."

I patted her hand. "I will," I said. "I will."

"And then get her some help. It's too late for me. I've carried this around for too many years —"

"It's not too late," I said, horrified that she would think that.

"Yes it is." She smiled bitterly. "I'm the only one

who knows that, who can say that. But Jory's young
... you could help her. Don't leave it till it's too
late."

I said nothing. There was a terrible sadness
about Polly, a bleakness, a sense of finality that
chilled me. I felt totally inadequate to respond to it.

"This is a shitty world for kids," she said, drying
her eyes on the sleeve of her turtleneck. "What kind
of a place is it where little girls have to beg their
own fathers not to hurt them? I said, 'Please, Daddy,
no. Don't.' What good did it do? None." She
shrugged. Then after a moment, her lips set in a
grim line, she said, "Let's get Ratliffe. Let's make
sure he pays."

"Whoa!" I said, concerned. "I'll get him. I will.
Your part is to take me there."

"Why ... don't you want help? I could help you."

"Listen to me," I said. "When you get to the
point where you hurt so much that you have to say
no or break in two, then you'll be ready. Ready to
help *yourself*. Then ready to learn how to be helpful
to other women. How to be strong for them. But
you're not there yet. Saying no ... it's a private
thing. You have to come to it on your own."

"So I have to help myself first?"

I squeezed her hands. "Or let someone else help
you. Then you can share yourself with others who
need you."

"Maybe," she whispered. "But maybe not. I'm not
... strong. I never have been."

"You'll find strength if you need it," I told her.
"What you have to find first is enough rage to say

no. And then you forge your own determination. Like the poet said: 'To strive, to seek, to find, and not to yield.' "

"Determination," she said, considering the concept.

"Yes. My friend Gray says it's the tiger's heart."

She said nothing, considering that or other things. I sat and watched her. Poor Polly. But try though I might, I couldn't think of anything to say to make her hurt less. Suddenly, outside, the moon rose over Ciel Island, bathing everything in light. I looked closely. The wind had died — the ocean looked like a smooth sheet of black silk, shot here and there with ripples of silver. This was it — the break in the storm.

"Come on," I said, taking her hands and pulling her to her feet. "Let's go strike a blow for our side. Let's go get Jory."

WEDNESDAY

Chapter 11

In the eerie hush, we walked down the brick pathway across Polly's back lawn to the boathouse. The rain had stopped, and the wind was just a gusty memory of what it had been. Clouds scudded across the face of the sky like a flotilla of ships under full sail, and when the last ragged galleon passed, there was the full moon, shining like a new dime. Our shadows were sharp-edged and inky black against the boards of the dock, and beneath our feet the weather-beaten wood looked like platinum. I watched as the dark shapes of Lester, Gray, and

Polly filed aboard the Whaler — as unlikely a trio of rescuers as had ever been assembled. Who were they anyhow but people who wanted to help? Looking up at the pitted, implacable face of the new moon, I suddenly felt very humble. Who was I to have such fine companions? The final lines from Tennyson's "Ulysses" came to mind:

"Death closes all: but something ere the end,
Some work of noble note, may yet be done ..."

Yes, I thought. Isn't that what really matters after all — to have found something worthwhile to which to lend one's skill, strength, and determination? To be able to say, when death closes all, that you strove mightily? And in that instant, I knew that I would never give up doing what I did — helping people in trouble. And for that reason, I would never go back to working for Niall. I needed to be my own boss, to decide who I would help and who I wouldn't. Tonia was wrong: I wasn't a courage junkie. But I loved — maybe beyond all other things — the moment when I walked out to face down the devil, knowing that I was absolutely, unassailably right and knowing too, that my wits, strength, and guts might not be enough. It wasn't courage I was hooked on — it was curiosity.

I laughed out loud and Lester turned, surprised.

"Nothing," I told him. "Carry on."

I stayed behind on the dock while Gray, Lester, and Polly boarded the little craft. A muffled growl told me that Polly had fired up the engine.

"Cast off!" she called over the muscular bass of the inboard motor.

I untied the lines and leaped aboard, using my foot to shove the boat away from the dock. Gray and Lester had taken seats on opposite sides of the boat, silent and unmoving, their bodies dark shadows. I went forward to join Polly and she pointed dead ahead.

"Ciel. We'll be there in ten minutes. I'll tie the Whaler to what's left of the Ratliffe's dock, in the little bay with the bell buoy. Then we —"

"Then you'll wait for Gray and me," I interrupted her, trying to sound authoritative. "Against my better judgment, I let Lester come along to keep you company. But neither of you is to set foot off the Whaler."

"I thought —"

"Don't, Polly," I warned her. "This is my fight — I told you that. You've made it possible for me to get to Ciel, and I'm very grateful to you for that. But from now on, it's all up to me."

"You *are* taking Gray along," Polly reminded me. "Well, we're going to have a little discussion about that too," I muttered. "Gray says she can get me through the tunnels and find Ratliffe for me, and I'll need that. But once she's done that, once I know where he is, I want her to get the hell out of there."

"How can Gray *know* that Jory and her dad are in the old mine?" Polly asked petulantly. "The Ratliffe's summer place is still usable. Don't you think —"

"I don't know how Gray knows anything," I confessed. "And I wouldn't dream of asking her. All *I* know is that I believe her. She's ... she's Gray. A damned Asian witch," I said softly, laughing again at the memory.

Polly looked shocked and turned away. Giving the Whaler a little more power, she brought it across the last few hundred yards of dark ocean to the entrance of a small bay. A bell buoy floated just outside the bay and its clanging and intermittently flashing light seemed oddly familiar to me. But I was far too wired to try to recall where I had seen it.

Polly cut the motor and the boat drifted to the dock. I jumped from the swim platform onto the rickety boards and caught the lines Lester threw me. Trying off to the cleats on the dock, I straightened up and took several deep breaths.

"Be careful," Polly called from the Whaler's stern. "That dock looks really rotten."

Gray climbed agilely from the boat to the dock and I noted with interest that she carried a coil of bright yellow nylon line over one shoulder.

"How long do we have?" I asked Polly.

She raised her face to the sky. Above us, the moon still blazed through gaps in the clouds but it seemed to me that they were bigger and thicker. And was it my imagination, or was the wind a little stronger? Behind us, out to sea, the tide was on the ebb and the waves hissed as they retreated down the pebble beach. As I looked at the silver phosphorescence of foam, I shivered a little, memory pricking me again.

"Mel said about six hours. I guess we have five left. He says the next storm looks like a real bitch." She shoved her hands in her parka pockets and looked belligerent. I was not happy about this new side of Polly. Evidently she was ticked off about something and I was afraid I knew what it was.

Evidently she wished that she, not Gray, was coming with me. Her identification with Jory was becoming a pretty scary thing.

"Okay," I said. "Listen up, you two. If we're not back when the weather changes, get on back to Thetis. We'll hole up in Ratliffe's place." Polly had told me that it was just out of sight, in a clearing past the crest of the cliff. I could see the wooden stairway rising from the dock to the top of the cliff, and I figured that from there we could find the path leading to the house. "We'll be back as quick as we can," I said, hefting my backpack.

"Good luck," Lester called.

Polly said nothing.

I shrugged. "Come on, Gray," I said. "Let's get this over with."

We were taking a short cut to the mine — a footpath that led along the clifftop for a quarter mile or so and then snaked its way down the cliff to a ventilation "window" in the mine's second level. A favorite entry point for Thetis youths who didn't mind trespassing in order to party in the abandoned mine, it was, Polly had explained, a narrow and dangerous access route. That, of course, was why the local kids loved it. We watched for our landmark — three tall cedar snags and two short ones, thrusting up at the night sky like broken fingers — and once we'd found it, we prepared to scuttle down the cliff face.

"This is a glorified goat trail," I groused to Gray, clutching bushes that grew out of the cliff face on my left. "Besides, it's so overgrown with vegetation, we'll be lucky if we don't trip and fall into the sea." I sneaked a peek at the ocean below us and it was not an inspiring sight. Fifty feet straight down, a half-dozen toothy Volkswagen-sized rocks had been exposed by the outgoing tide. Falling onto them would not be fun.

"Then we must be careful," Gray said, ever the soul of common sense. "Turn and face the cliff if you think you cannot keep your footing."

I did, and that was all that made the climb bearable. The footpath was no more than two feet wide at its widest point, and so rocky and treacherous that a straight-ahead descent was impossible. Finally, however, we came to the ventilation window. A metal grate set in the rock at head-height, the mesh was old and rusted and came away easily when I tugged. I set it down by my feet and slipped off my backpack. Fishing for my flashlight, I poked my head into the ventilation window and shone the light around. It was not an encouraging sight. I guessed there had been a cave-in here not too long ago because piles of rubble covered the floor. In this particular passage, though, the ceiling was at least six feet high and I breathed a sigh of relief. We hadn't the time to crawl on our bellies.

"I'm going in," I told Gray and wriggled head first through the opening, letting myself down slowly to the floor of the passage inside. Gray passed me my backpack and wriggled through behind me. I set the timer on my digital watch and looked at Gray. The moon shone in through the ventilation opening, making a square of silver on the floor and I was unpleasantly reminded of how much this rocky chamber reminded me of prison cells in old movies. Or tombs.

"There is no place for imagination underground," Gray said, as though she were reading my mind. "Let us resolve to go quickly into the entrails of the earth, do what must be done, and travel back quickly to the light. This is only rock, and we shall be in it a very short time."

"Right," I said doubtfully. "You better lead. You're the one who knows where she's going."

Gray reached into her pack and took out a slender wand-like piece of plastic, about six inches long. With a snap, she bent it double and it immediately gave off a ghostly green light. She placed it atop the highest piece of rubble, about ten feet from the ventilation window. "A beacon," she said. "Now, come, let us find Jory."

That was easier said than done. We climbed over, around, and through piles of rock rubble, wriggled through passages where we had to crawl on our stomachs, and knocked our heads and skinned our hands over and over on the unforgiving rock. Things that squeaked and scuttled fled as we approached and more than once my flashlight beam illuminated rodent-sized white skeletons. The farther we went into the earth, the danker and colder it became, and I had to clamp my jaws together to keep my teeth from chattering. Finally I checked my watch — we had been at this for over two hours, and not once had Gray paused or faltered. She seemed to know exactly which way to turn. As for me, I hadn't a clue. If she was following the trail they made in the fallen rock, she was a very skillful tracker indeed.

But where had she learned such skills? I was watching the soles of Gray's boots, thinking such thoughts, when, suddenly, she began to move backwards very fast.

"Light out!" she whispered urgently. I thumbed my flashlight off and in the total darkness, Gray scuttled backwards to join me. "Voices," she whispered very close to my ear.

At last. "Where? Can you tell?"

"Yes. Ahead and to the left. This passage joins another one, a larger one. They are there. There is a light. Also, someone is cooking."

"All right," I said, thinking very fast. "I'm going on. You go back and wait for me at the ventilation window."

"You will not find your way back there alone," Gray said reasonably.

Shit. She was right. "Wait here then," I told her.

"Very well," she agreed.

This was too easy. "Please, Gray. I need to know where you'll be."

"I will be here."

Why did I doubt her? Shoving my flashlight in a pocket of my jeans, I crawled on elbows and knees to the junction of this passage and the next, larger one. Sure enough, just as Gray had said, there was drone of speech from someplace away to my right, and very faintly, the glow of a light. I took a deep breath, rose to a crouch and, hugging the wall of the tunnel, crept toward the light.

In the glow of a lantern, Jory sat hugging her knees, her back to the tunnel wall. Ratliffe sat opposite her, cooking bacon in an iron pan on a Coleman stove, using a hunting knife with a blade of truly awesome proportions. Every so often he would look over at Jory, *tink* the blade against the side of the iron skillet and chuckle. Between Ratliffe and Jory lay two sleeping bags, zipped together. I felt my skin crawl. What was this anyway — the bridal bed? Forcing myself to stay calm, I unzipped my jacket and reached for my .357. This was going to be a piece of cake, I told myself, bringing the gun around in front of me. I'd get myself in between Jory and Ratliffe and ...

A blonde-haired figure in a navy parka burst out of the darkness behind Ratliffe and it took me several heartbeats to realize it was Polly. She carried what I saw was the Whaler's flare gun and as if things were happening in slow motion, I saw her bring the gun up and aim it at Ratliffe's head.

No! I cried silently. It was wrong, all wrong. She was too damned close to him, and besides, she hadn't given him any instructions, gotten his attention. And the knife ...

He looked at her slack-jawed, then in a gesture I could have predicted, he came up off the tunnel floor and threw the knife at her. There was one instant when he could have chosen not to throw the knife but say, to tackle her or knock her down, but he didn't make either of those choices. I saw him *choose* to throw the knife. He was evidently aiming for her chest, but must have overestimated his throw, because the knife took her in the throat. She dropped the flare gun and fell to the tunnel floor without a sound, an amazed look on her face, both hands on Ratliffe's knife.

"You bastard!" I yelled, leaping forward, kicking Ratliffe's legs out from under him. He fell like a toppled fir and as he scrambled to get his legs underneath him, I kicked him again. In the head this time. He subsided with a *wuff*, which bought me enough time to look at Polly. The knife had taken her just above the collarbone. One quick glance was enough to tell me that there was nothing I could do for her. Her eyes were terrified and she held onto Ratliffe's knife as her life poured out around her fingers. She struggled with bubbling, choking breaths, drowning slowly, horribly in her own blood.

"Just relax," I lied, brushing her hair back from her forehead. "You're going to be okay."

She nodded once, and opened her mouth to say something.

"Sweetie, save your strength," I said through my tears.

She frowned, and raised one bloody hand toward me. I bent close. "No," she whispered. "No."

I clutched her hand very tightly, tears streaming down my face. "Yes," I told her. "You said no. For Jory." And for Polly too. You finally said no for Polly. *No, Daddy, please.* God, how many more Pollys and Jorys did there have to be?

She closed her eyes.

"Well now, that's awfully touching," an amused voice said. "Before I start bawling, why don't you get up and turn around."

I did. Kirk Ratliffe stood facing me, a shotgun in his hands. "You need to put some more oomph into your kicks," he chuckled. "Women. None of you knows a goddamned thing about fighting. Toss that gun over here before you hurt yourself," he said, pointing to the .357 that dangled from my hand.

I felt very, very tired. "No," I said.

"No?" he said, incredulous. "Then I'll just have to shoot you."

"You won't!" a husky voice yelled from behind him. "I'll shoot *you* with this thing if you hurt Caitlin. You let her go!"

Oh, Jesus, not again. As Ratliffe moved his head a fraction to bring Jory into view, I dived for the nearest pile of rubble. Skinning my knees, scraping my face on the rock, I rolled into a ball and scuttled into the darkness.

"Jory, get away! Run back down the tunnel! Gray's there!" I yelled, counting on the fact that Ratliffe wouldn't shoot his own daughter. I peered out from behind my boulders to see Jory, flare gun held out in front of her, backing away from Ratliffe, retreating down the tunnel. When she turned and ran, I cheered silently. Now it was me and Ratliffe.

He made a strangled, inarticulate sound and took a step after her. I steadied the .357 on my left arm, sighted, and shot him in the right shoulder. He stumbled, howled like a beast and turned back to me, raising the shotgun.

"Come on, Ratliffe," I taunted, "pick on someone your own size. Come get *me*. If you can."

He aimed the shotgun at my hiding place and I flattened myself behind the boulders, pressing my scraped cheek to the cold, clammy floor. And as I did so, I felt ... what? ... a trembling, a shuddering in the rock beneath me. A growling. Mystified, I placed my left hand flat on the floor. Then the ground began to move underneath me and I knew what was happening.

"Cave in!" I yelled, jumping to my feet. "The damned mine is collapsing, Ratliffe!"

The floor gave a heave, and I fell to my knees. Just as well, for Ratliffe would have blown me in two had I stayed upright a moment longer. I heard the *boom* and felt the shotgun pellets fan the air above my head. Then, heedless of the fact that he still had one more shot, I stuffed my gun in my jeans, staggered to my feet and ran after Jory down the passageway. Or tried to. Another convulsive lurch of the earth knocked me to the ground and I realized that I probably wasn't going anywhere. There was a dull *whoomp* somewhere up ahead of me and my eardrums felt as though they had been blown into my head. I clapped my hands to my ears, yelling in pain, and tried to stagger to my feet. The lantern that had lighted Ratliffe's cozy little den had been extinguished in one of the earth's heaves and in the pitch dark, I had no idea which way to run. But still, I had to try. Ahead, I thought. Ahead. Rising to one knee, I tried to get my feet underneath me but slipped and fell into what seemed to be half a foot of cold water. Water? An atavistic dread gripped me, and I plunged my hand into the water and tasted it. It was salty. The sea was flooding into the mine!

I opened my mouth to yell, to say hell, no, I don't want to drown, when a cold wave of water snatched me off my feet and carried me along with it down the passageway. The mine behind me must have already collapsed, I guessed, and the sea was now racing in, filling the passages and tunnels. I saw with crystal clarity that what was left of the mine would slide into the sea, too, unable to bear the weight of all that water. And when it did, it would carry me with it.

There was no point in even trying to resist. I just concentrated on protecting my head as the water tumbled me down one passageway after another. With a crunch that drove my breath from my body, I was finally slammed into a pile of rubble, putting a temporary end to my wild ride. Groaning, I reached out with both arms to embrace the rock, and screamed. My right arm, which had been smashed against the cavern wall in one of my tumbles, simply refused to work. The pain in my forearm was so intense I suspected it was broken. So I grabbed the rock with my left hand, hoping to save myself from being swept on down the passageway and, gasping and choking, clambered up the rockpile until I was safe. Wiping the salt water from my eyes, I asked myself: now what? This was surely just a temporary respite. In a minute or an hour the water would rise, plucking me off my perch and sending me on my way. Something warm trickled into my eyes, and I wiped my forehead, my fingers coming away sticky with blood. I was sure I looked the way I felt — as though I had gone three rounds with the Terminator.

I laid my head on my outstretched arms, wondering how long I could cling here, or even what the point of it all was. I was so hurt, tired, cold, and wet that my brain wouldn't function. Why was I bothering? Why should I struggle anymore? As far as I knew, Jory had made it to safety. And Ratliffe? He and I were now rattling round down here like ingredients in a blender. And in another few minutes, I was sure the controls were to be turned to MINCE. So why fight? Why not just let go.

As I shifted position, trying to take the weight

off a badly bruised knee, I saw, unbelievably, off to my right, a light. Something that gave off a pale greenish glow. Jesus, no, I thought. It can't be. Gray's beacon? That meant I was directly opposite the passage that led to the ventilation window! How in hell had I gotten back here?

Think, nitwit, I told myself. I had a chance, although admittedly it was a slim one. If I could just get out of this main passageway and into the side tunnel I could escape by the ventilation window. But that was a mighty big if.

Suddenly, the rush of water around and past my perch just ... stopped. And there was silence. Total, absolute silence. I drew a ragged breath. Something — combination of mud and rock somewhere behind me — must be temporarily acting like a plug, damming the flow of water. I didn't even wait to wonder how long it was likely to hold. Instead, I scrambled back down the rockpile and leaped into the icy water. There was hardly any current at all and I waded through the knee-deep brine into the side tunnel, making straight for Gray's beacon. Almost there, I told myself as I stumbled over rocks hidden beneath the water, almost there. And then I saw it — the ventilation window! I was going to make it after all, I thought, as I stumbled forward.

A hand gripped my arm and for one crazy instant I thought it was Ratliffe. But it wasn't. In the wash of moonlight through the opening, I recognized Gray.

"Why aren't you someplace safe?" I croaked. "Did Jory make it?"

Gray smiled faintly. "Jory is safe with Lester.

And I am here as I said I would be. Come, we must hurry."

"Go through first," I told her. "You're going to have to help me, though. I think my arm is broken."

Gray wriggled through the window, lowered herself to the path outside and handed me a coil of yellow nylon rope. "Tie this around your waist," she said.

I tied myself off and tucked my right arm against my body. Putting my left arm through the opening, I tried to wriggle through. But my legs wouldn't cooperate. Now that salvation was almost at hand, they had simply quit. They felt boneless, rubbery, useless. "Jesus Christ!" I yelled, trying to pull myself through with my left arm alone.

And then I heard it — a roar that sounded like four locomotives advancing up the tunnel behind me. The temporary dam holding back the water must have burst and now the sea was rushing in. It would fill every tunnel and passage of the mine, spurt out through every opening, and carry everything into the ocean. And if I didn't hustle my ass through the ventilation window, it would take me with it.

"Caitlin!" Gray said urgently.

Half in, half out of the ventilation window, I looked at her anxious face. And remembered something. A bargain I had made kneeling in the mud beside Gray's van. I had promised whatever goddess I prayed to that the next time I got into a scrape, she could have me if only she would spare Gray's life. And she had. I swallowed and looked at Gray again, suddenly realizing what I had seen the night I had been lost in the fog. The woman with my face who had walked into the moon had indeed been me. I had seen my own ghost. I had seen myself dead.

"I can't," I babbled. "I promised. Get away. Save yourself."

"Foolish one," she chided me, and grabbing my jacket with both hands, she pulled me out of the ventilation window. "You did not buy my life with yours. I chose to return. I am the one who must always return."

I landed in a heap on the trail and she hauled me to my feet again. Grabbing the yellow rope that tethered me, she dragged me up the path away from the window. Not a moment too soon, for behind us, with a roar, the sea burst from the ventilation window in a spew of water, rock, and mud. Pure, absolute terror inspired my flagging legs and I staggered to my feet, lurching and stumbling after Gray as she pulled me up the path. At the top I saw, improbably, that Jory was waiting.

"Why aren't you on the boat with Lester?" I croaked, falling to my knees.

She set her chin in defiance. "I wanted to help."

"Take Caitlin's left side," Gray instructed her.

With Jory on my left, Gray on my right, and me like a lead weight between, we somehow navigated the clifftop path. Then we stood at the stairway leading down to Ratliffe's rickety dock and the Whaler. Salvation. *Polly*, I thought in a spasm of pain, *oh, Polly*. Then my legs gave out, the world spun away, and I slid into darkness. "Sorry," I told them as I slipped away. "Sorry."

*   *   *   *   *

I awoke on the Whaler, lying on the deck, a boat cushion under my head, a blanket wrapped around me. Jory sat beside me, knees drawn up to her chin. Overhead the stars still blazed, but I could see the steady buildup of clouds. The wind had risen, whipping the sea into waves and the Whaler bucked and *splatted* against every one, sending red rockets of pain through my arm. "Who's driving this thing?" I asked Jory.

"Gray."

"Why not?" I replied. What couldn't Gray do? I thought about sitting up but the pain in my arm decided me against it. "How are you?" I asked.

She looked at me evenly. "Not so good."

"Me neither," I told her. Then, after a minute, I remembered. "Hey, I've got something for you," I told her. "Reach into my right-hand jeans pocket. There's a buckskin bag in there." I rolled on my side and she slid her hand into my pocket. "Go ahead, look inside."

She held up a tiny stone carving of a wolf. "What is it?"

"It's a gift from your great-grandmother. Jonna's grandmother. She was a full-bloodied Iroquois. Her French name was Fleur. She gave me that twenty-two years ago and told me I would know what to do with it when the time came."

Jory closed her fingers over the totem. "How do you know this is the time?" she asked in her husky croak.

I closed my eyes. "I just know."

"I ... I ..." Jory stammered.

I opened my eyes to see tears running down her face. "Why am I alive when that woman, Polly is dead, and my mother is dead, and you, you almost died —" She broke off, sobbing.

I propped myself on my left elbow. "Come here, Jory."

She threw herself into my arms and awkwardly, I patted her back.

"I ask those questions too. They're tough ones, that's for sure."

"Oh, you're awake," a voice said. Lester staggered out of the Whaler's little cabin. "We'll be there soon."

"Where?" I asked, momentarily confused.

"Where? Why, Thetis, of course."

Ah yes, Thetis. Polly's home. "Jory, help an old lady stand up."

Jory helped me to my feet and I stood with my left arm around her shoulder, leaning on her.

"Are you okay?" Lester asked.

"Right now, no. I probably will be later, though." In fact, I felt decidedly odd. Maybe it was the tumbling I had taken in the mine, or the pain in my arm, but I felt strangely ... disembodied. A little like a sleepwalker. Thinking of the vision I had seen in the fog, I shivered — it had been so real. And Gray's dream, her so-called memory of the future, it had seemed real, too. If they were real, what did that mean — that I was dreaming now? But how was I to know? How were we to ever know which was the dream and which the reality?

"I'm sorry for what happened. To Polly," Lester said, his eyes sparkling with tears.

"So am I. But I think we'd do her death a

disservice to cry for her. She chose that path. It was her way of saying no. I don't think she'd want us to weep. Let's find some way to celebrate her heroism instead. She did 'some work of noble note' before she died."

He took off his glasses and wiped his eyes. "Okay. But what about us? What did we do?"

"Us? We did what we could. We fought the good fight. That's all anyone can ask. Now we have to carry on."

"With what?" he asked, his voice breaking.

"With the struggle, kiddo. What did Tennyson say:

"Come, my friends,
Tis not too late to seek a newer world.
Push off, and sitting well in order smite
The sounding furrows, for my purpose holds
To sail beyond the sunset and the baths
Of all the western stars, until I die."

"A newer world," he said. "I like that. Poets always say things best. But I didn't know you were, like, into all those lofty sentiments."

"Well, I am," I told him. "What else gives all this mess any meaning?"

He was silent for a moment, clearly thinking. "Not much. Self-sacrifice. Doing what's right. Beauty. Love, maybe. Aren't those the things that count?"

"Indeed they are," I told him. "Indeed they are."

Also available from Silver Moon Books

DIVING DEEP—Erotic Lesbian Love Stories
Edited by KATHERINE V. FORREST and
BARBARA GRIER

SILVER MOON'S first short story anthology brings
together stories of love, desire, romance and passion.

From authors such as Nikki Baker, Lauren Wright
Douglas, Karin Kallmaker, Lee Lynch, Isabel Miller,
Robbi Sommers, Phyllis Horn and Jeane Harris come
stories of lust, vengeance, initiation and anonymity.
Here are characters who want to revise their pasts and
change their futures; women on opposing sides who
find novel ways of trading; above all women who are
not afraid to discover and use the depths of their
passion.

A sizzling collection of erotic stories – lesbian love from
authors who know how to please.

ISBN 1 872642 14 4   **£6.99**

Silver Moon Books

Publishers of Lesbian Romance, Detective and Thriller Novels

UNDER THE SOUTHERN CROSS, CLAIRE McNAB
Claire McNab departs from her famous Detective Inspector Carol Ashton series to bring her readers this passionate romance set against the majestic landscape of Australia.
(£6.99, 192pp, ISBN 1 872642 17 9).

CRAZY FOR LOVING, JAYE MAIMAN
Romance and mystery with detective Robin Miller loose in New York. Jaye Maiman at the top of her form in this sequel to the very popular *I Left My Heart*.
(£6.99, 320pp, ISBN 1 872642 19 5).

PAPERBACK ROMANCE, KARIN KALLMAKER
Literary agent Alison, romantic novelist Carolyn, and the enigmatic conductor Nicolas Frost – who is *certainly* not what he seems – come together in this fast moving, erotic lesbian love story.
(£6.99, 256pp, ISBN 1 872642 13 6).

THE GARBAGE DUMP MURDERS, ROSE BEECHAM
A monster is on the loose – his victims a grisly jigsaw puzzle of anonymous body parts left around the city. Set against him is Amanda Valentine, a tough and unusual cop. Unpredictable, passionate and, as adversaries and lovers quickly learn, very much her own woman.
(£6.99, 240pp, ISBN 1 872642 15 2).

LOVE, ZENA BETH, DIANE SALVATORE
The novel all lesbian America is talking about. The story of Joyce Ecco's love affair with Zena Beth Frazer, world famous lesbian author. Zena Beth is sexy, witty, outrageous and recovering from her sensational love affair with sports superstar Helena Zoe. A passionate novel of love and jealousy which has the ring of truth.
(£6.99, 224pp, ISBN 1 872642 10 1).

CHASING THE SHADOW, LAUREN WRIGHT DOUGLAS
As the action builds to its nerve tearing climax Caitlin Reece must face a moral dilemma which nearly costs her her life. A hard-hitting and hugely entertaining thriller which packs a heart-stopping sting in its tail.
(£6.99, 224pp, ISBN 1 872642 09 8).

COP OUT, CLAIRE McNAB
A bestseller from this very popular author. The story of the Darcy family – a family at war – and the killer who menaces it. Can Carol Ashton find the murderer before it is too late?
(£6.99, 191pp, ISBN 1 872642 08 X).